D1061703

THE TWELFTH JUROR

A man stands accused at the Old Bailey of the wilful murder of his wife. The charge cannot be more serious, yet to those around him the prisoner in the dock seems surprisingly self-assured; calm, collected and arrogant. Appearances can deceive, however, and even counsel for the defence does not know of his client's inner turmoil as the accused watches the jurors take their oath. For what can these men and women, strangers all, know of his past, his motivations, his private world? And are some of them perhaps too willing to prejudge him guilty—or innocent?

THE TWELFTH JUROR

B. M. GILL

A New Portway Large Print Book

CHIVERS PRESS
BATH

JAN 1 4 1986

First published 1984
by
Hodder and Stoughton Limited
This Large Print edition published by
Chivers Press
by arrangement with
Hodder and Stoughton Limited
and in the U.S.A. with
Charles Scribner's Sons
at the request of
The London & Home Counties Branch
of
The Library Association
1985

ISBN 0 85119 333 1

Copyright © 1984 by B. M. Gill
All rights reserved

British Library Cataloguing in Publication Data

Gill, B. M.
  The twelfth juror.—Large print ed.—(A New
Portway large print book)
  I. Title
  823'.914[F]   PR6057.I53/

  ISBN 0–85119–333–1

Photoset, printed and bound in Great Britain by
REDWOOD BURN LIMITED, Trowbridge, Wiltshire

JAN 1 4 1986

THE TWELFTH JUROR

PROLOGUE

I swear by Almighty God that I will faithfully try the several issues joined between our Sovereign Lady the Queen and the defendant and a true verdict give according to the evidence.

Juror's oath

Twelve members of the public, peremptorily summonsed to jury service at the Old Bailey ('whereof fail not as you will answer the contrary at your peril'), are about to take the juror's oath at the trial of Edward Carne, television presenter, who is accused of murdering his wife, Jocelyn.

Most of them would prefer to get on quietly with their own lives. Others will enjoy the experience. Some will be worried and distressed.

They will react to the challenge and interpret the evidence according to their temperaments. All are fallible. Some know it and are afraid.

They are:

Thomas Leary, aged fifty-nine, bachelor. Irish by birth, he has resided in England for twenty-four years. Profession: Professor of Classics at King's College, London.

Sarah Gayland, aged twenty-seven, unmarried. Originally from Yorkshire. Works as secretary

1

to a dentist in Harley Street.

Peter Lomax, aged thirty-three, married. Recently appointed assistant to the head carpet-buyer of a leading London store.

Colin Middler, aged forty-six, married. He and his wife run a private chiropody practice.

James Cornwallis, aged sixty-four, widower. Self-employed plumber and central-heating contractor.

Irene Sinclair, aged fifty-seven, spinster. Worked as an interpreter for a firm of exporters. Now retired.

Selina McKay, aged forty. Married to a medical practitioner. Two sons. Trained as a gemmologist and designs costume jewellery.

Trina Thompson, aged twenty-four, but looks much younger. Cohabiting with a social worker. Teaches in a nursery school.

Sam Jacobson, aged forty-eight, married. Three young daughters. Owner of a licensed snack-bar.

William Dalton, aged forty-five, widower. Worked for some years as a mining engineer in South Africa. Now unemployed.

Elaine Balfour, aged fifty-three. Widow of a Northumbrian farmer. A Londoner by birth, she returned to the city on her husband's death.

Robert Quinn, aged thirty-eight, divorced. One young son. Worked as a journalist on *The Times* before being made redundant. Runs a squat for four young buskers.

THE TRIAL

CHAPTER ONE

The clerk of the court addressed the defendant:

'Prisoner at the Bar, the names of the persons I am about to call are the persons who will form a jury to try you. If you have any objection to them, or to any of them, you must make your objection as they come severally to the Book to be sworn and before they are sworn, and your objection shall be heard.'

'Fire away,' Carne said. It was an unfortunate choice of words and lacked respect. He wore his television personality like a second skin and couldn't shake it off, especially now that he was again on public display. Panic, anger and despair boiled inside him like a witch's brew, but none of it showed. Had he been tied to a stake in front of a firing squad he would have looked just as bland, felt just as terrible. In that situation the words would have been apt.

'I do beg your pardon,' he said, 'please do proceed.' It sounded deeply sarcastic, but wasn't intended to be.

Roy McNair, the defending counsel, was careful not to catch the judge's eye. Mr Justice Spencer-Leigh believed that the moronic majority owned television sets and that the intellectual minority despised the medium. The judge made a virtue of never having seen any of Edward Carne's programmes. Carne, until recently television news announcer and presenter of *Arcadia*, an arts programme in a country setting, had a large and for the most part enthusiastic following of viewers. Several hundreds had been queueing for seats in Number One Court since six o'clock, and the first-comers who had determinedly stayed on during the dawn downpour were now seated, damp, tired but pleased, where they could have a good view. The court smelt of wet mackintoshes. The July sunshine had broken through the clouds by nine-thirty and the crowds had grown again and were becoming a traffic hazard. More police had been called in to control them. The judge disliked being upstaged and McNair knew it. Both he and Carne's solicitor, John Richardson, had warned Carne during the several interviews they had had with him to shed his television personality and emerge an ordinary mortal.

'Inarticulate, gauche and scared witless?' Carne had suggested.

'Just remember that the only television coverage you'll get will be when you enter and leave court,' McNair had replied brusquely. 'There won't be any cameras trained on you inside. It may be your show, but you're not running it, and any errors you make won't be conveniently disposed of in the cutting-room. There won't be a prompt screen, or whatever it's called, if you don't know what to say next. You may not be fighting for your life, but you are fighting for your freedom.'

'They are, of course,' said Carne, 'one and the same. Incarcerate me and I'll die.'

'It could take an uncomfortably long time,' McNair pointed out without sympathy.

Carne smiled wryly. 'As my defence counsel you should give me comfort and support.'

'I shall support you although you make it difficult for me when every remark you make sounds flippant, and from your attitude I find it hard to believe that you need comfort.'

'Oh, but I do,' said Carne, 'believe me, I do.'

The horror of remand at Brixton had stripped pounds off him, but he had had several pounds to lose and didn't look the worse for it. He could have just returned from a rigorous walking holiday where the rations were meagre and the terrain rugged. The reality was like a black cloud in his head—a noxious cloud that smelt of urine. At night when he had managed to sleep at all he had dreamt of a cyanide capsule under his tongue; the dream had become a nightmare when the capsule, hard and slippery, had refused to break. To be condemned to death was bearable. To be condemned to life imprisonment was not.

There was, of course, the possibility of

5

acquittal. Those twelve people whose names were being called as they entered the jury box might declare him innocent and let him go. It was his prerogative, he had just been told, to object to all or any of them. On what grounds could he object? They had been selected by ballot in open court, like picking Bingo numbers. By what power of intellect, intuition or wisdom could they judge him? Twelve others might do better. Or worse. He was afraid of them. He despised them. Looking at them, he felt extremely angry, and so he looked away.

I object, he thought. I object. *I object!*

McNair, sensing his tension, went over to him. 'Do you know any of them?'

'They're a cross-section of my television public. They all know me.'

'An occupational hazard. I doubt we could find twelve who don't.'

'Thank you.' The twisted, amused smile. The eyes bleak. Carne fingered his blue and grey striped tie; a correct, rather funereal tie which suited the occasion. He hadn't had to buy a tie for years. They arrived, often anonymously and usually at Christmas, together with other gifts.

'Do you,' McNair persisted, 'for any valid reason, object to any of them?'

'I object to the fact that twelve people who don't know anything about me are about to play God over me.'

'Is that all?'

Carne looked at McNair in astonishment.

'Just remember,' McNair said quietly, 'that you're here on a murder charge. Leave the jury to me. If anyone plays God, it's the judge. Don't antagonise him.'

Mr Justice Spencer-Leigh, crimson-clad and looking like a gaudily feathered cockerel, was already seated in majesty when Carne had been brought up to the dock. The court officials, in black and white plumage, occupied lower perches in the hierarchy. It was like an Orwellian take-off of one of his own shows; all it needed was music. His last *Arcadia* programme had been set in one of the richest farms in Britain. The barn, about the size of the courtroom, was strewn with scrubbed-looking straw, the colour of honey. Tubs of geraniums had been placed around the door and a local harpist excited by the prospect of national television coverage played gentle bucolic tunes. Here, the judge had a posy of flowers, necessary in the Newgate days to mask the stench but now just a quaint custom, and all the players looked suitably grim.

The clerk of the court had read the charge:

'Edward Graham Carne, you are charged on indictment that during the period of the second and the third of August of last year you feloniously, wilfully, and of your malice aforethought did kill and murder your wife, Jocelyn. How say you, are you guilty or not

7

guilty?'

'Not guilty.' An emphatic denial.

And now a bunch of incompetents were being chosen to consider the veracity of the plea. It was like being flung into a deep and sinister ocean where amateurs frolicked. If they pushed him under would they know why? Would they consider every point before abandoning him? Was there one sweet chance in hell that they might haul him out?

He watched them curiously as they took the oath.

Thomas Leary held the Bible in his right hand and read the juror's oath from the card. 'I swear by Almighty God that I will faithfully try the several issues joined between our Sovereign Lady the Queen and the defendant and a true verdict give according to the evidence.'

Carne saw a man in late middle-age, with a ruff of white hair surrounding a bald freckled cranium. He wore a hand-knitted sweater in two shades of blue under a grey flannel suit. His Irish accent, though slight, was ominous. One of the most vicious reviews of the *Arcadia* programme had been penned by an expatriate Dubliner, and Carne wondered whether they might be one and the same person.

The next five jurors came and went quickly, making for the most part only a peripheral impression on him. He correctly slotted Sarah Gayland into the secretary category: a young

8

migrant from the north, plump and pretty and silently proclaiming her CND sympathies by a badge worn prominently on the lapel of her maroon jacket. For a moment Carne allowed himself a surreal and manic fantasy as he imagined the jury turning on each other in a vociferous battle about unilateralism. Then his thoughts returned to the more mundane as he scrutinised Peter Lomax and Colin Middler in turn, the next two individuals to be sworn in. Lomax showed his resentment as he swore the oath. He was missing a carpet-buying trip to the Middle East and his disappointment sounded in his voice. Each word pinged like shrapnel and Carne could see the prejudice glowering out of him. A Cassius character, he thought, lean and treacherous. Colin Middler, softly spoken and personally unassuming, was annoyed at the thought of the money he could be earning at his private chiropody practice. But unlike Lomax he didn't allow his annoyance to show.

Then came James Cornwallis and Irene Sinclair. Cornwallis didn't like what he regarded as religious clap-trap and resented taking the oath. His wife had died two years previously and the local vicar had refused to conduct the burial service because the family were non-attenders. Cornwallis had got his own back during the winter freeze-up when the vicar's pipes had burst and he had refused to mend them. That was justice. Carne, deceived by his mild

9

exterior, dismissed him as a nonentity.

Irene Sinclair had been pleased when she had discovered the nature of the case. It would be one of the best publicised trials of the year. She read the oath with authority and, after handing the Bible back to the clerk, smiled at Carne. He had delivered her from tedium and she was grateful. Carne, startled by her smile, didn't respond. He fingered his tie and wondered if she had sent it.

The next juror to be called was Selina McKay. She read the oath and then held the Bible a moment thinking about the words. Almighty God tripped off the tongue easily enough, though she wasn't in the habit of invoking Him. The courtroom had the look of a church, but none of the ambience. At least the judge no longer called the blessing of God on an act of judicial murder. That blasphemy had been removed. Carne wouldn't hang. She refused to let her mind dwell on the alternative.

Carne, aware that she reminded him of someone, looked at her intently. She was in early middle-age, tall and fair and dressed in a summer-weight suit of dark blue with a high-necked white blouse. She was an older version of the Swedish journalist he had had an affair with many years ago when Jocelyn was pregnant with Frances. It had been an act of betrayal at a time when Jocelyn had needed special care and tenderness. He wished the memory hadn't come to him now. Jocelyn dead was a black area in the centre of his imagination—a fact he dared not define. Soon that dark area would take shape. During the course of the trial it would be fleshed out and clothed. She would become alive in his mind, and he would hear her voice again.

He began to shake.

Watching Trina Thompson take the oath calmed him a little. She was obviously nervous and muttered a panic stricken 'Oh, Christ!' when she realised she'd taken the Bible in the left hand instead of the right. Were jurors called this young? Carne wondered, sympathy blending with amusement. She looked about the same age as Frances, who was nineteen. They both wore similar spectacles—large, tinted and, in Frances's case, non-magnifying. He had been the favourite parent when she was small. In her teens she had turned to Jocelyn. She looked like Jocelyn. Small and stubby, with dark brown eyes and thick short hair. The humour that had calmed him a minute or so ago began bleeding out of him again.

Eight jurors had been sworn in: there were only four more to go. Carne hoped fervently that none of them would make him think of Jocelyn and Frances again. And indeed the ninth juror, Sam Jacobson, although an imposing figure, evoked memories of no one. The big and burly snack-bar owner didn't want to be here today, but accepted the fact that he had to be. He

11

scowled when the Bible was handed to him, but asked meekly if he might swear on the Pentateuch, and did so with his head covered.

In contrast, William Dalton, small and thin and with a habit of running his left hand through his sparse ginger hair, appeared innocuous. His voice with its squeezed South African vowels was low as he read from the card. For him Carne personified British decadence. He hadn't seen him on the box but had read enough about him to pre-judge him. He shot him a glance across the court which Carne rightly interpreted as one of contempt.

Up in the public gallery a woman spectator had a paroxysm of coughing which went on for several minutes. Acutely embarrassed, she made her way out. Carne's throat felt raw with nervous reaction. If he had a spasm of coughing he couldn't just get up and go. He closed his eyes and swallowed convulsively.

Elaine Balfour, prevented from taking the oath until the woman had removed herself, read it at last in a light and pleasant voice. 'I will faithfully try the several issues,' she promised. Under the guidance of a benign God, she hoped, who would know more about it than she did. Attendance at Harvest Festival was about the extent of her religious observances, but she believed in a force for good which made the potatoes grow and generally looked after things. She didn't want to hurt Carne, but if he had killed his wife ... ? She kept her head averted, careful not to look at him.

Carne, his nerves once more under control, opened his eyes as she handed the Bible back. Glimpsing only her profile and carefully styled grey hair he was unable to form any opinion. He had scrutinised and appraised each juror in turn with varying degrees of interest, but still didn't know what to make of them individually or collectively. But as he heard Quinn, the twelfth juror, exchanging remarks with the judge, he sensed a joker in the pack and felt uneasy.

Robert Quinn was breaking the law by being there. A refusal to serve would have been accepted by the court. When the summons had been received a few weeks ago he had no valid reason to opt out, but in the meantime circumstances had changed. During the last hour when he had discovered that he was to serve on the Edward Carne case he had wondered if he could feign sudden illness and get away with it. He decided he couldn't. Here he would be pitting his wits against wits more keen.

His reluctance to read the oath wasn't obvious. It sounded like a theatrical performance, delivered in a voice rich and commanding, and quite at variance with the way he looked. Whilst all the other jurors had dressed with some care for the occasion, Quinn's patched jeans and open-necked shirt were blatantly casual.

The judge spoke for the first time. 'Solemn words, Mr Quinn.'

'Quite awesome, my Lord.'

'To be spoken with sincerity.' The warning was implicit.

The jury sat in two rows of six. Thomas Leary, the first juror, was at the end of the first row and farthest away from Robert Quinn who was diagonally opposite behind him. Leary knew Quinn. That resonant voice was unforgettable. Craning around to take another look at him he tried to slot him into the right background and period of time. He was in his middle to late thirties so not a contemporary of the Dublin days. One of his students of ten to fifteen years ago? Oxford? Yes, Oxford. The memory suddenly became very clear. Quinn on a mescalin trip. Roaring and weeping about the sacrifice of Iphigeneia and then taking off into the dark in the guise, apparently, of Agamemnon. The following morning Leary had found his pet cat Tibbles asphyxiated on the back seat of Quinn's car which was parked adjacent to his. A length of tubing was connected to the exhaust and the engine had obviously been running for a long time. That Tibbles should have become Iphigeneia and been sacrificed was easier to believe than that she had arranged her own suicide. He had pointed this out to Quinn with considerable

14

anger and pain. Quinn hadn't denied it. Later that same day Quinn had removed himself from Oxford for good. The loss of a sharp intellect was a pity, but Leary had grieved for his cat more. Moving awkwardly in the cramped space, he leaned backward for a closer look.

Quinn, remembering him in that instant, hastily looked away. He had no recollection of actually killing the cat, but knew that he had done so. The fact that it was only a cat had been a relief to him. Not that he had anything against cats apart from their urinating on his orchids and sitting on his statuary. His orchids were housed in a broken-down greenhouse and his statues, like grubby little graveyard angels, were dotted around his backyard, constant reminders of a classical education quite literally gone to pot.

He chanced a cautious look at Leary, who had stopped inspecting him, and saw his face in profile. The young professor had become an old professor rather faster than he should. That's what the academic life did for you, it leeched on to your arteries. At some stage during this trial he supposed they would have to acknowledge each other. Everybody in the course of time would be forced to talk to everyone else. The huge ape of a man, smelling of garlic and sitting pressed up against him on his left, was making shy rumblings preparatory to saying something to him now. He waited.

'If you wouldn't mind very much, sir,' Jacobson whispered, 'I'm getting a cramp in my leg. I need to put it out. If we could change places, and I sat on the outside, it would be better.'

'By all means.' Quinn stood in the aisle. Jacobson passed him like a huge furtive pugilist and Quinn took the seat he had vacated.

The judge, about to make a scathing remark about musical chairs, refrained. The jury were here because they had been told to be here. They deserved a degree of courtesy. For an indefinite period they would sit in reluctant contiguity. Eventually they would become like one large family, a family of misfits, but with one common cause. He hoped that they would behave with reasonable good sense and that no one would be anti-social in any unpleasant way. Eventually, he hoped, they would arrive at the right verdict.

CHAPTER TWO

Gordon Breddon, QC, rose to make his opening speech. He was an experienced barrister who always prepared his briefs with meticulous care and rarely lost any sleep over them. Last night, however, he had been awake into the small hours, his mind busy with the events of the coming day. The Edward Carne trial might not be the most important of his career, but it would be the first to thrust him into the limelight.

'My Lord,' he inclined his head to the judge and then turned to the jury. 'Members of the jury. I appear for the Director of Public Prosecutions. As you have already heard in the indictment, the defendant, Edward Carne, is charged with the wilful murder of his wife, Jocelyn. He has pleaded not guilty. If the Crown succeeds in proving the case—beyond all reasonable doubt—the defendant will be found guilty of murder within the meaning of Section Six of the Homicide Act.' He paused and looked over at Carne, and then turned to the jury again. 'It is my duty, as a dispassionate representative of the Crown, to lay the facts before you and to assist you in discovering where the truth lies. It is your duty to listen carefully to the evidence and then, in the course of time, decide whether or not the charge of murder against Edward Carne has been proved to your complete satisfaction.' Breddon put a special emphasis on the last two words, and paused briefly before continuing. 'I shall commence by giving you an outline of the events that led up to his arrest.'

The killing of Jocelyn Carne had already had immense coverage both in the newspapers and on television. The word 'alleged' held up like a talisman against accusations of contempt had been used freely. All wording had been circumspect, but a lurid word-picture of Carne had been painted with skilful strokes full of carefully monitored innuendoes.

The jury and the spectators in the gallery who knew most of it already sat back in expectation of hearing the details they didn't know.

Carne, in the dock, began to feel oddly disassociated from everything. He noticed that his brown leather shoes needed to be cleaned. To maintain a reasonable degree of personal freshness was impossible in Brixton. Polished shoes were an unattainable luxury. The prison issue wouldn't look like these. Certainly they wouldn't feel like these. He had been wearing hand-made shoes for years. They would take them away from him. He would be like a child stripped bare. To the skin. Not even his own underwear. The final bloody indignity of prison-issue underpants and socks. He had been shocked when his bail had been terminated just before the trial. Had they expected him to abscond? Or cut his throat?

Gordon Breddon turned and looked at him. 'One of our golden performers of television,' he said drily. He let his glance linger for a full twenty seconds before turning back to the jury.

'How many of you, I wonder, as you look at Carne, believe you are looking at an old friend? Over the past five years he has read the news to you, like another living presence in your home. Together you have shared world disasters and

18

triumphs. His voice, his expression, have conveyed emotions suitable for every occasion. Controlled emotions. As a newsreader it was necessary that he should show no obvious bias. You could form your own opinions as you watched him and believe, if you wished, that he shared them with you. To the solitary his was the voice and the face that brought a kind of companionship. No word out of place. Nothing said to shock. He posed no threat to the family. Three years ago the country programme *Arcadia* was launched. He emerged from the confines of the newsdesk and did his own thing. All very pure. Country crafts to a background of Chopin's *Barcarolle*. Land reclamation or bird watching or punting on the Severn with a little ballet here or a trumpet voluntary there. All very good. In fact, excellent. Good, clean, British television.' He was careful to iron the sarcasm out of his voice when he turned to Carne again. 'I congratulate you on it. And I mean that quite seriously. You, under the guidance of your production team, were doing a good job.'

Carne nodded politely. That Breddon was honing up the sword edge before plunging it he knew well enough. He had the look of a conquistador—strong features, swarthy skin. A voice like iron filings.

'At this point,' Breddon proceeded, facing the jury again, 'it will help you to understand the underlying psychological complexities of the case if I give you a brief biography of the defendant. Edward Carne was born forty-six years ago in a suburb of Liverpool. He attended a local grammar school, but failed to make any particular mark for himself there. On leaving school he had a job as a clerk in a shipping office and for a hobby took part in local repertory. It was here that he met Jocelyn Davenport. Two years later they married. I must ask you to cast your mind back to the early sixties when the marriage took place. The old moral values were beginning to be eroded, but not very much. There was an engagement and a wedding in church. No trial period of living together. Jocelyn worked in a Liverpool bookshop. She and Carne had shared interests, in acting and the arts generally. A year after their marriage their daughter Frances was born. She is now nineteen and the Carnes' only child.'

Breddon paused. 'A child sometimes keeps a marriage together, but it would be conjecture if I were to tell you that this was the case with the Carnes. As the trial proceeds you will hear from various witnesses who will give you factual evidence relating to the state of the marriage. For my part I will now continue to give you a general broad outline of Carne's life from the Liverpool days when he was a poorly paid clerk until he attained television fame and a correspondingly comfortable bank balance.'

The judge interrupted. 'Twenty years is a long time. Is all this necessary?'

'I believe it sets the scene, my Lord, and makes clearer subsequent events.'

'Very well—if you must.'

Breddon had all the facts at his fingertips and had no need to glance at his sheaf of notes. They were necessary for his junior, Arnold Forbes, who would do some of the more routine questioning of witnesses later. His own memory was excellent.

He carried on: 'Picture, if you will, a young father with a seemingly safe but boring job. And then the shipping company runs into difficulties. The job folds. Carne is out of work for six months. Jocelyn takes a secretarial course and gets a temporary job. For a while she supports the family and Carne looks after the child.'

Carne looks after the child, Carne repeated to himself. What was Breddon trying to show— bitterness at the role reversal? There hadn't been. He had enjoyed being at home with Frances. They had amused each other with infantile trivia. He had taught her to read. The house had been sordidly untidy and the meals erratic, but none of it had mattered.

He forced his attention back to Breddon.

'Eventually Carne manages to get taken on by another shipping company, but this time in Bristol. The family moves. The job lasts for several years. During this time Jocelyn helps out whenever money is tight. She is an excellent wife—most supportive. Their hobby, the local repertory company, doesn't pay them anything, but they can indulge their pleasure in it without being out of pocket.' Breddon glanced towards the dock. 'Carne has an exceptionally good speaking voice and is no mean talent as an actor. A BBC producer based at Bristol meets him at one of the theatrical get-togethers. When Carne is thrown out of a job for the second time—no fault of his, shipping was in the doldrums—the producer pulls a few strings and gets him an appointment in local radio. Radio is a fairly anonymous arts medium—apart from the few well-known performers—so at this stage there was no great change in life-style.'

Spencer-Leigh made a point of looking at his watch, but this time said nothing. Breddon ignored him.

'Seven years ago the family moved to London. Carne was still working for radio and then he was tried out as a newsreader on television—with instant success. He looked good on the box. He sounded good. The public liked him. The peak of his career was reached with the programme *Arcadia*. Financially in a comparatively strong position, he was able to afford a pleasant Victorian terraced house, not too far from the BBC, and a country cottage in Snowdonia. He began to socialise. He and

Jocelyn were asked out a great deal. At first they went as a couple, but as time went on she began refusing invitations.'

Breddon squeezed his lower lip between finger and thumb as if deep in thought. 'It would be wrong to jump to a hasty conclusion about her solitariness. Perhaps she was shy—or socially inept. Or too hurt, perhaps, by her husband's growing and quite overt interest in other women. She may have seen the cottage in Snowdonia as a peaceful retreat from a way of life she didn't like—or as a bolthole from a troubled marriage. She went there frequently— but she always returned. She hadn't deserted Carne. He had no grounds for divorcing her. He could give her grounds—adultery many times over. Witnesses will attest to this. Everything I'm telling you is factual and relevant to the case.'

Carne moved uncomfortably. He felt like a spectator in a video show—a reluctant observer of an old film. My life as others see it, he thought bitterly. Factual? Oh, yes. Some of it.

Breddon looked up at the public gallery and then over at the jury again. When he resumed his voice was cold and level. 'Frances, the Carnes' daughter, attended a day school and must have felt the chill of the domestic environment. A few months before her mother's death, she became a student of modern languages at Liverpool University. By now,

Carne, with both wife and daughter off the premises for a lot of the time, had a regular mistress, of whom you'll hear more. His relationship with the actress, Hester Allendale, wasn't discreet. It would have been impossible for Jocelyn not to have known about it. We can only guess at her reaction and we're not in the business of guessing. Perhaps she was a tolerant woman. Perhaps she was a strong believer in the marriage bond and refused to break it. When Jocelyn went to the cottage in Wales last summer, Carne was working on a programme set in Devon. Just before the programme ended Carne told the producer he had to return to London. Jocelyn was still away. On the night of the third of August, a day after Carne left Devon so precipitately, the cottage was gutted by fire. Jocelyn's car, in a shed across the yard, was a burnt-out wreck. According to the fire officer the car was put on fire first and then the arsonist set the cottage ablaze. Welsh arsonists tend to concentrate on cottages rather than cars. The area is remote and there was ample time for the fire raiser to do a thorough job. Still—the sequence was odd. And why no slogans? At the time, however, it seemed likely that it was the work of Welsh extremists who disliked, perhaps with good cause, having their cottages bought by the English at prices the villagers themselves couldn't afford. The fire was first seen by a local shepherd about seven o'clock in the morning.

He alerted the police who in turn got in touch with Carne in London. Or attempted to. When Carne didn't answer the phone call at a little after eight, they tried again later. It was nearly midday when they made contact. He enquired about his wife. The police reassured him that there was no body on the premises. Carne's wife had been seen in the village a couple of days before the fire. She hadn't been seen since.'

Breddon took out his handkerchief and dabbed at the corner of his mouth. It was a strategic pause and he let his eyes linger on each member of the jury in turn before carrying on.

'For several weeks the mysterious disappearance of Jocelyn Carne made news. A thorough search of the area was made, a search for Jocelyn in which Carne joined. Winter closed in. It was a bad winter, you'll remember, with heavy snowfalls, and the search was abandoned. The thaw came in late December, just after Christmas, and with it came an anonymous phone call directing the police to look in an area just off a mountain track and not far from the cottage. There, the caller said, was where Carne had hidden the murdered body of his wife.' Breddon's voice deepened and he spoke more slowly. 'The police, following the caller's directions, found the remains of a woman. Judging by the extent of the decomposition, she had probably been dead about four months—since August. The fire, you will remember, occurred in August. There was no evidence of burnt flesh or charred clothing. The body had not been in the fire. Her death, according to the pathologist, had been caused by blows to the head by a sharp instrument and her skull had been fractured. Dental records established identity.' He half-turned on his heel so that he had his back to the jury and was facing Carne. 'The woman was Jocelyn Carne.'

Carne looked away and began pushing at the cuticles of the nails of his left hand. He felt nauseous.

Breddon, after ten seconds of silence, spoke to the jury once more. 'Her grave was a narrow aperture about eight feet deep, covered with gorse. Her body lay face upwards on heather. A perfect hiding place. It's possible she would never have been found if that anonymous call hadn't been made to the police at the local village police station. The phone call came from a telephone kiosk, but the exact location of the kiosk wasn't traced. The caller—a woman— could be an accessory to the crime. As witnesses give their evidence you will draw your own conclusions. It is necessary to bear in mind the time lapse between the murder and the phone call—approximately four months. Was the caller's conscience very troubled during that time? Or had she only recently become aware of the facts? How Carne reacted to the finding of his wife's body you will hear from Chief

Superintendent Hallam, the officer who called on him at his home and accompanied him to Wales.'

He turned to the judge. 'If your Lordship agrees, I should like to call the police witnesses after the luncheon recess, so that there should be no break in the continuity of their evidence.'

Mr Justice Spencer-Leigh had no objection, and the court rose.

*   *   *

The jury, like a theatrical audience, strolled out into the main hall where the statue of Elizabeth Fry presided, hand on heart.

'Lovely ceiling,' Irene Sinclair said to Elaine Balfour. It was somehow comforting to speak to another juror of the same sex and about the same age. *'Poise the cause in justice equal scales'* she read from the inscription under the mural at the far end.

Mrs Balfour said there were restaurants on the premises. Should they go and look for one of them? On holidays, if one travelled alone, one made tentative gestures of friendship to other single travellers. The situation couldn't be more different, but the need for sociability felt the same. She noticed that the young girl, the scared little rabbit as she thought of her, was making her way out with some speed. She wondered if she would come back.

Robert Quinn had also made his way out speedily before Professor Leary could catch up with him. There was a small licensed restaurant five minutes away which served grills at a reasonable price. The place smelt of cooked meat and coffee and his gastric juices got going in anticipation. He gave his order for steak and chips and sat at a corner table well away from the window. It had been Blossom's turn to cook him his breakfast and she had burnt the bacon. There hadn't been any more and he had been forced to make do with toast.

He had started his meal and was eating hungrily when the tall, fair jurywoman brought her tray over to his table. 'Do you mind if we share? All the tables are full.'

He stood up politely and said he didn't mind. She introduced herself. 'Selina McKay.'

'Robert Quinn.'

He noticed that she had a mixed green salad with a small portion of cheese and was drinking grapefruit juice. A disciplined figure. Good features and a nice voice. If she wore her hair down there would be a lot of it.

She was analysing him, too. A few years younger than she was. Too old to trail the tattered remnants of adolescence by mocking the oath. If he had been. Perhaps he always declaimed like that. On a soap-box at Hyde Park Corner? On a West End stage?

'I suppose you could have affirmed,' she said.

It took him a minute or two to follow the drift. He smiled, but didn't answer.

She sipped her grapefruit juice, aware that she had trespassed. The topic was tender.

'Who are we,' she said, 'to judge Carne?'

He looked at her in surprise. 'According to recent amendments to the law, the jury is as driven snow. Not a single felon amongst us.'

'Then it doesn't worry you to have power over someone else?'

'Our power,' he reminded her, 'is divided by twelve.' Or, in this case, by eleven, he reminded himself. His own position on the jury was precarious.

This morning he had let events take him along. This afternoon he could continue walking in the wrong direction—back into the Old Bailey—or he could do the sensible thing. The choice worried him. Frowning, he concentrated on his steak and chips and wondered what kind of a meal Carne was being given.

She speared a piece of tomato. 'His lover, Hester Allendale, has been talking very freely to the newspaper men. It must be prejudicial. She's even dropped hints about inside information. Do you suppose she was at the cottage when it happened?'

His own source of information might tell him, he mused, given time. He said it was possible. 'She'll deny it, of course.'

'Naturally.'

Selina McKay sensed that he was reluctant to discuss the case. A perfectly proper reluctance in a good juryman, she thought.

★　　　★　　　★

During the afternoon session Breddon called a succession of police witnesses. Their evidence was given in sequence. First, the burning of the cottage, then the search for the missing woman. The air in the courtroom was heavy and hot. The evidence was detailed, repetitive and dull. Some of the older jury members felt on the verge of sleep. The oldest, Cornwallis, twice almost nodded off.

Carne, watching them, felt a mixture of anger and despair. Even McNair, his defending counsel, was leaning back in his seat, his eyes half-closed, questioning nothing.

As yet there was nothing to question.

Interest, like a small cool breeze, was aroused when Constable Williams took the stand. It was he who had received the anonymous phone call. At first he'd thought it was a hoax. Breddon was inviting him to tell him about it. They were a polite lot up here in London, but he doubted if they would remain polite if he told it exactly as it happened.

Sergeant Jones had primed him to give his evidence properly and so far he had taken the oath and given his name and number very smoothly. 'The call came through in the afternoon,' he told Breddon. 'I was doing some paperwork. Sergeant Jones was investigating a traffic offence in the main street. I picked up the telephone and a woman asked if she was speaking to the village police station. I said yes . . .'

Breddon stopped him. 'You made notes of the telephone conversation?'

'Yes, sir.'

'You have those notes with you now?'

'Yes, sir.' (Edited version—the first lot were scribbled on the back of a betting slip.)

Breddon asked for permission for the notes to be read. It was given.

Williams took out his carefully written notes, stewed over by himself and the sergeant. The traffic offence had been the sergeant's invention. He had been in the bog but that hadn't sounded right.

'At fourteen-thirty hours on the twenty-seventh of December, 1982, a phone call was received from a woman speaking from a call box. She claimed to have knowledge of the whereabouts of the murdered body of Jocelyn Carne. The dead woman, she stated, had been buried by her husband in a grave of heather two miles up the Bryn Eglwys path near the sheep shelter. She further pinpointed the locality by saying that it was within a few yards of the standing stone on the western side of the path.

31

When asked to reveal her identity the caller rang off.'

Williams returned the notebook to his pocket.

'Obviously not a verbatim report,' Breddon said.

'There wasn't time, sir, to take it down as it happened. It was more important to get the location right.'

'You didn't attempt to keep her talking while the call was being traced?'

'There was only me there, sir, and anyway she rang off too fast.'

'Pity,' said Breddon. He had a pretty good idea of what had happened. A sleepy little police station had had what amounted to a bomb hurled at it. The constable and sergeant had been concussed into disbelief and then they had gathered up the fragments and done the best they could with them.

'Can you describe her voice, Constable?'

'It was an English voice talking, sir, not a Welsh voice talking English.'

'Did she sound calm, or upset?'

'Oh, very calm, sir. She knew what she was talking about.'

'Yes—obviously. What did you do next?'

'I told the sergeant, sir.'

Breddon didn't ask what the sergeant had said. The truth, he imagined, would be amusing but not helpful. He thanked him and sat down.

McNair stood up. 'My learned friend asked

you to describe the caller's voice. You said it was an English voice speaking English, not a Welsh voice speaking English. You have a good ear for accents?'

'Yes, sir.'

'Do you detect any regional accent in my voice?'

'No, sir.'

'It would surprise you, then, to know I'm a Scotsman?'

'You keep it under very good control, sir.'

There was a ripple of laughter and McNair smiled. 'Was the voice on the telephone a deep voice, or a high voice?'

'I'm not sure, sir. An ordinary voice.'

'The Welsh are a musical people—would the person you listened to on the phone be a soprano—a contralto—or even a tenor?'

'A tenor is a man, sir,' Williams said, amused.

'Quite. The timbre of the human voice has a wide range. The masculine voice and the feminine voice can sometimes sound almost the same. A contralto and a tenor might be indistinguishable at the other end of a telephone. The caller didn't identify herself—or *himself*. It's possible you jumped to the wrong conclusion.'

The jury had it firmly fixed in their minds that Hester Allendale had made the call; he hoped he had un-fixed their minds just a little. 'The call,' he told Williams, 'could have been

33

made by a man.'

He sat down before the constable could dispute it.

The sergeant's evidence, which followed, dealt with the abortive effort to trace the call and with the search for the body. They hadn't expected to find it and had been shocked when they had. He hadn't seen a decomposing body before and hoped he'd never see one again.

The final police witness during the afternoon session was Chief Superintendent Hallam. He told the court he had called on Edward Carne to give him the news about finding his wife's body.

'It was eleven-fifteen in the morning. The defendant was still in bed. Mrs Hooper, the housekeeper, showed me into the drawing-room and went to call Carne. He came down in his dressing-gown and apologised for not having dressed. I told him who I was, and before I could say anything more he said, "Good God— has anything happened to Frances?" He explained that Frances was his daughter. I told him that I hadn't come about his daughter, but about his wife. I told him that her body had been found, but not about the phone call accusing him. He asked where it had been found. I needed to consult my notes to be accurate and read from them. He suggested that she must have fallen.'

Breddon asked about his emotional reaction to the news.

'He had been upset at the possibility of something having happened to his daughter. Apparently she'd had a couple of minor accidents in her car. It was difficult for me to gauge his reaction to the news about his wife. I told him I would accompany him to Wales so that he could identify the body. He said he would have to inform the BBC—that he was due to attend a rehearsal in the afternoon.'

'How would you describe his reaction?' asked Breddon.

The chief superintendent answered that it had struck him as surprisingly cool. 'He made the phone call to his producer from another room. I don't know what he said. He then went upstairs to dress. Finally he called his housekeeper and told her in my presence that Mrs Carne's body had been found. "If Frances should come," he said, "tell her I've gone to the cottage."'

'Was he still very worried about his daughter?'

'He was afraid she might read the news in the papers, or see it on the television. I asked him where she was so that she might be contacted. He said that she'd opted out of university—that there had been a family row. He hadn't seen her for some weeks. She had left her last address in Liverpool and hadn't given him her new one.'

'During the drive to Wales did Carne speak to you about his wife?'

'No. We spoke very little. He suggested that

we should stop at a small inn just outside Shrewsbury for a snack. Constable Snape was driving and he directed him down some minor roads until we reached the inn. It was a very wet day. Carne remarked that the worst thunderstorm he had ever experienced had been the previous summer in the Caernarvonshire mountains.'

'So he talked about the weather?' Breddon raised his eyebrows. 'A very cool customer.'

Carne, leaning forward in the dock, remembered the drive very clearly. He could even smell the rain. The dark Shropshire earth oozing with wetness—the constable's damp mackintosh—small globules of water on the superintendent's tweed overcoat. The inn sign had been flapping in the gusting wind. A log fire burned brightly in the saloon bar. The sandwiches on the bar counter were freshly made. He had chosen ham and pickle. The beer, as always, was good. The two police officers had drunk coffee. He had said something to them about drinking and duty and could he tempt them to have something stronger—on him. It had sounded facetious. He hadn't meant it to. Being calm was living on a different level of consciousness. You cut out what you couldn't tolerate. You were free of it, sometimes for hours on end. During those respite periods your heart thumped quietly and steadily, you breathed normally, you ate ham and pickles and drank beer and watched the rain running in rivulets down a pub window.

He had lost the last few exchanges and noticed that McNair was on his feet.

'I suggest to you,' McNair was saying, 'that if a guilty man were being driven to the scene of a crime his attitude would have been different. Carne was shocked. My learned friend called him a cool customer. I would prefer to describe him as a man not yet fully aware of the meaning of loss. Had he been guilty he would have anticipated the possibility of the body being recovered. He would have rehearsed his reaction. He would have put on the kind of unrealistic performance you seem to have expected. When you are informed of the sudden death of someone you love, you don't weep. It's something you can't, at first, believe. The pain of grief comes later. Carne talked about a thunderstorm in Wales. A guilty man would have eulogised about the virtues of a wife much loved. When you're concussed you feel nothing. It's only later, when you revive, that the pain comes. You were driving to Wales with Carne so that he could identify his wife's body. He didn't perform for you. He wasn't a cool customer. He was a man behaving with total honesty.'

Mr Justice Spencer-Leigh told McNair to get on with his cross-examination of the witness and McNair retorted rather too brusquely that he had been making a point. He underlined it by asking the chief superintendent if he had ever gone on a five-hour drive with a bereaved husband under similar circumstances before.

'No, sir.'

A safe answer to a safe question. 'Then take my word for it,' McNair said emphatically, 'that Carne's behaviour wasn't in the slightest degree unusual.' He sat down.

So, I'm being normal now, Carne thought, for the time being quite without feeling. He wondered if the jury were reacting more favourably to Breddon or to McNair.

The most recently bereaved member of the jury was Cornwallis. He had been putting in a new bathroom for a customer when the police had called to tell him that his wife had suffered a heart attack in the shopping precinct. It had taken them several painful moments to admit that she was dead. The bathroom suite was a pale pink, like diluted blood. He still couldn't stand the colour. His immediate reaction had been to sit on the side of the bath and not believe a word of it. McNair had been right about that. Later, when he had made the identification at the hospital, he had begun to believe it. That night he had played his cassette of bird songs in the shed at the bottom of the garden, because he couldn't bear to go into his house. Was that the same thing as talking about the thunderstorm? Nature violent, or nature sweet, seemed necessary in times of grief. But had Carne been grieving? He looked at him, frowning, and came to no conclusion.

The judge, aware that minds were sharper when the day was young, decided to call a halt to the proceedings. The jury would need to exercise their powers of concentration when listening to the forensic evidence. He suggested that as the afternoon was well advanced no more witnesses should be called.

Carne watched the judge bowing himself out and then he was taken below. Without him, the dock was like a switched-off television set. There was a strong feeling of anti-climax.

CHAPTER THREE

'We meet again under most unusual circumstances,' Professor Leary said, holding out his hand to Quinn.

They were standing outside the Bailey, hedged in by the crowds who were hoping to catch sight of Carne being driven back to Brixton.

Quinn shook the proffered hand without enthusiasm.

Both men had memories of Quinn's inglorious and dramatic last day at Oxford. Once more Leary mourned the death of his cat, but didn't mention it. Quinn, wondering if an apology or a denial would be in order, decided not to mention it either.

The professor hid his animosity behind a smile. 'It seems we're once more in a disputatious situation, unless the evidence should prove incontrovertible.'

If an academic career made one talk like that, Quinn thought, then hooray for the mescalin trip. 'Poor bastard,' he said.

Leary was surprised. 'You have sympathy for Carne?'

'Naturally. Haven't you?'

'Certainly not. I hope my mind is totally unbiased and receptive.'

'Like a plate washed under a tap,' Quinn suggested, 'shining clean and ready for the dollops of evidence to land on it. Commendable.'

'Not an analogy I'd have chosen,' Leary made an effort not to lose his smile, 'but true. I didn't want to be called for jury service. It's extremely irritating to have my routine interrupted, but I shall discharge the onerous duty to the best of my ability.'

'I'm sure you will.' Quinn's smile was sardonic.

Many years ago, during a tutorial, the professor had had a strong urge to give Quinn a sharp clip around the jaw during a tense situation. Time should mellow one's emotions. It didn't. He asked him suavely what career he had followed after being sent down.

'I left,' Quinn said. 'Freely.'

The police van with Carne draped in a blanket was turning into the street. There was a clicking of cameras and the crowd surged forward. Quinn, like a surfer making good use of a wave, allowed himself to be carried along. Leary, more frail, hadn't any choice. They were pressed up tight on the pavement's edge as the throng bayed. And then a few fans cheered. The van roared off and the crowd began to thin.

'So you believe he's innocent?' Leary asked.

'I didn't say that. I said I felt sympathy for him.'

'If he should be proved guilty, how will you feel then?'

Quinn looked at him coldly. 'If you and I sent him to rot on a life sentence, how do you suppose I'll feel? Self-righteous? Pleased with myself?'

'Punishment,' Leary said, quoting St Augustine, 'is justice for the unjust.' He reminded Quinn that he hadn't answered his earlier question about his career.

Quinn told him shortly that he ran a squat.

'You *what?*'

'My house was taken over by a group of buskers while I was in Germany last year, and I let them stay.'

It was a convenient arrangement, but one that the professor could never understand. Quinn had been settling Gretl and their young son Timothy into their flat in Frankfurt and had stayed on for a while. The divorce had been amicable. Gretl came from a wealthy family of brewers and didn't need alimony. Timothy didn't need maintenance. At ten, he didn't seem to need his father, either. Quinn loved him enough to mind and too much to make a nuisance of himself. He had returned to London, feeling desolate, to find four young itinerant musicians in his home. They had expected to be slung out on to the street; instead he had sat on the frayed Aubusson rug with them in the shabby living-room and drunk what was left of the vodka. That night he had slept with the Chinese girl, Blossom, in the guest bedroom.

He tried to explain. 'Their busking buys the food. They take it in turn to cook it. They sometimes clean the house. They chip in with the cost of heating. In return they get the place rent free and they're not harassed by the police. It works very well.'

Leary was looking at him blankly. 'And you—what do you *do?*'

'On hot days,' Quinn said, 'I sit in my back yard and admire my orchids. On cold days I sit inside and practise hedonism.'

The passing traffic was noisy. Leary wasn't sure if he was hearing correctly, but nevertheless came to the reluctant conclusion that he was. It was quite reprehensible, so why did he feel such a strong pang of jealousy?

'What did you do,' he persisted, 'before you started doing nothing?'

Quinn told him that he'd been a reporter on *The Times*. 'I, along with quite a few others, was expendable.'

Now here was a situation the professor could understand and sympathise with. Quinn, his former student, had for a while at least been respectable. He had worked.

'Too bad,' he said.

'Too bad for too long,' Quinn agreed.

The crowd had thinned now and it was possible to get away without fighting for an exit. The evening papers were on sale. He took himself off with a brusque, 'See you tomorrow,' and went to buy a couple.

He wondered how Frances Carne would react to the reporting of her father's trial. She was behaving like a small animal with its head down a hole. Occasionally she pulled it out and had a drink. Occasionally she cried. When Nils, the big shaggy-bearded Swede, had been busking outside Euston station three days ago she had gone and sat beside him—too pissed, he had explained later, to stand up. He had bought her coffee and offered to take her home, in a taxi if necessary—it had been a good day. If she went home, she had told him, the police would force a subpoena on her. She had been eluding them for weeks. Nils hadn't been sure what a subpoena was, but guessed it wasn't pleasant.

'And so, Robert,' he had said, 'I brought her home to you.'

He had stood with her in the hall like a large gun-dog presenting him with a bedraggled pheasant. Quinn, not pleased, had been about to say so when she lurched past him, crawled up the stairs, and went to sleep with her head on the top step. Timothy's small bedroom was empty. He told Nils to put her there. 'And don't lay her,' he warned. 'She's probably under the age of consent.'

He had expected her to leave for home, wherever that was, the next day when she'd slept it off, so her reluctance to do anything other than sit around and nurse her hangover annoyed him. He wondered what the buskers had told her in the morning before he'd got up. Whatever it was she seemed to be preparing to take root on the strength of it.

He asked her who she was, where her home was and why didn't she go there.

Her answers surprised him. Annoyance gave way to compassion. He didn't have to touch her to feel the pulse of her pain.

He suggested that if she were called to give evidence it might help her father's case if she put in a few good words for him.

The conversation took place at the kitchen table. Blossom, or Lucille, had left a bag of potatoes ready to be peeled. She took one out of the bag and sliced it into small cubes on the table.

'No,' she said.

The action had Freudian overtones. Carne chopped up because he'd chopped up her mother?

He asked her how old she was and was relieved when she said nineteen.

Nils, he remembered, had picked her up at Euston station. Where had she been planning to travel? To—or from? Or nowhere? In a train—or under a train?

He enquired if she had anywhere to go—friends—relatives. She'd been around them all, she said, but hadn't felt at ease anywhere. The police could have traced her to any of the addresses.

He thought her fear of the subpoena exaggerated, but understood her state of mind well enough to be sympathetic. Timothy wouldn't be coming home on a visit for several months. He told her the room was hers for as long as she needed it.

She explained that her money had run out. 'Will it be all right to pay you later,' she asked, 'when I go back home?'

'Christ,' he said, 'this is a squat, not a hotel. If you feel you've got to do something then wash the dishes.'

In the morning, before leaving for the Old

Bailey, he had explained that he had been called for jury duty. 'But as there are twenty-three courts in constant use,' he said, 'the odds against my serving on your father's case are high.'

Luck, he should have remembered, was a fickle lady.

He drove home and parked the car on the square of concrete that had once been the front garden of the Edwardian terraced house. One of the street kids had been in and scrawled 'Tote' across it with blue chalk. Someone, probably Blossom, the only busker interested in flowers, had put a pot of petunias into a plastic Woolworth container and placed it by the front door. The blue paint of the door was peeling. He supposed he ought to do something about it. Since Gretl had departed with Timothy the house had been allowed to fall back into its original state of decay. It was an unlikely hide-out for the daughter of television's super-star.

He took the newspapers into the house and put them down on the sofa in the living-room. Frances was in the back yard pegging her jeans and jersey on the line. Lucille had lent her a yellow cotton skirt and a black shirt. The skirt was too long for her. She had hitched it up with elastic and pushed an orchid into the waistband.

He went to join her and pointed to the orchid in mock anger. 'I've nurtured that bloody bloom.'

46

'It fell off. It was on the greenhouse floor. I didn't pick it.'

Her speech was slurred. Later, if she followed the usual pattern, she would be blotto, thought Quinn. He guessed she was staying sober long enough to find out what had happened at the trial.

The buskers were out playing to the end-of-day shoppers before starting on the theatre queues. She passed on the message that Nils had left something in the oven. He wasn't hungry so let it stay there and instead poured himself a scotch. She followed him into the living-room and noticed the newspapers. Nervously her hands plucked at the orchid. A couple of petals drifted on to the rug.

A dive into an icy sea, when the dive couldn't be avoided, had better be made fast. He plunged into an account of the day's happenings at the Old Bailey, ending with: 'You were mentioned. Your opting out of university and the row with your father.'

She went to sit on the sofa and he sat beside her. The newspapers were between them, and both carried pictures of Carne on the front page. 'I don't know how full the newspaper accounts are. I haven't read them yet. I suggest you do, and I'll fill in whatever they've left out. You'll gather from all this that I'm on the jury.'

Her tinted glasses didn't disguise the shock and anxiety in her eyes. 'That means I've got to

47

go? I don't know *where* to go . . .'

He had been considering the various possibilities on the drive home. He was worried for himself and for Frances—but mainly for Frances—and had tried to consider the problem rationally. If she went, he would admit that he had met her and had only become aware of the relationship after the evidence of the first day. One day's contempt of court made in ignorance wasn't too heinous. Once she left him it would be unnecessary to divulge her address. He was short of cash, but he and the buskers between them might have sufficient for her to go to ground at a small hotel for a while. That would be the solution if she weren't so fearful of a subpoena and if she were in a better frame of mind generally. She needed a caring environment—someone to talk to. If she went he would be anxious about her. She wasn't his responsibility, but he felt responsible nonetheless. His conscience was selective. It always had been. He lived by his own laws. Staying on the jury seemed the lesser evil than kicking her out. By staying on it he might help her in some practical way. So stay on it and chance the consequences.

He told her she wouldn't have to go. 'The buskers won't talk. No one need know.'

She was sitting, half-turned from him, so that the newspapers weren't in her line of vision. Gratitude mingled with relief and was expressed

48

laconically. 'Thanks,' she said.

He finished his drink and went out to water the orchids so that she might look at the newspapers on her own. When he returned she had left the living-room and he could hear the tap running in the bathroom. The papers were crumpled on the sofa. The two photographs of Carne had been torn to pieces and thrown into the empty grate. He flicked his lighter and burnt them. That, he guessed, was what she would want him to do.

CHAPTER FOUR

On the second day of the trial the jury were beginning to find their way around. No one made the mistake of expecting to enter the Bailey by the main wrought-iron gates. These hadn't been used since an IRA bomb attack in 1973. They all walked confidently to the East Wing extension and went in through the swing-doors where the contents of handbags and briefcases were checked by X-ray machines. If someone wanted to shoot anybody nowadays, it wouldn't be easy.

Colin Middler, the chiropodist, alerted the machine with a pair of nail-clippers with a broken spring which he hoped to take for repair during the lunch hour. He displayed them rather sheepishly to the officer in charge and was nodded through. 'This trial is a disaster for the self-employed,' he said to Sarah Gayland who was stuffing the contents back into her handbag. 'How is it affecting you?'

Sarah said that she was salaried—secretary to a dental surgeon. The financial aspect didn't bother her. She had called in at the dental clinic on her way home yesterday and met her temporary replacement. 'She's good with the patients,' her boss had said. Good for Peter, too, Sarah had thought bitterly. She was a gentle-faced blonde with eyes as old as Cleopatra's in her prime. Peter had gone on to explain that his wife was up in town shopping for a few days, so not to expect him at her flat. Some young girls, she thought, worked pretty damned fast. She had spent the night alone, deeply suspicious and very depressed.

'There's more to life than money,' she pointed out to Middler. He agreed. 'But it buys freedom. I'm saving up for an early retirement.' It couldn't buy freedom for Carne, she thought, and his retirement could be spent behind bars. He was in a worse position than any of them. Misery was relative.

The court was due to sit at ten-thirty and Jacobson was very nearly late. He charged across the main hall like a Neanderthal man in pursuit of an enemy and only just made it with minutes to spare. One of his daughters was sitting a music exam and he had driven her to the building where the exam was being held. She was twelve years old and so far had failed every exam she had tried. He wondered who would suffer most this morning—Edward Carne or Esther. He hoped he would have the strength of will to think mainly of Carne.

With the arrival of Jacobson the jury were all assembled like a class of students in a new school. They smiled politely at each other and made desultory conversation. None of them mentioned Carne. That they should ever lose their inhibitions sufficiently to argue violently about him seemed exceedingly unlikely. Only Quinn could visualise the situation that far ahead and just now he preferred not to look at it.

Just before half past ten Carne was brought up to the dock. He felt grubby and tired. His sleep had been uneasy, disturbed by half-formed dreams like bats on a grey night. He glanced at the jury. They were all there. The public gallery was full. Frances was absent. Keep away, he thought. Keep on keeping away. Crouch behind your wall of pain wherever you are. Don't come closer.

McNair went over to him and outlined the probable events of the morning. 'Be prepared,' he warned him. 'It won't be pleasant.'

At ten-thirty-two there was the ritual procession and everyone stood as the judge entered. He bowed to the court and to the jury

51

before sitting. A shaft of sunlight struck across his crimson robes like a television spotlight. A good theatrical effect, Carne thought; he's even got the sun on his side.

The evidence during the first hour went more deeply into that given the previous afternoon. Gas chromatography had been used to identify the cause of the fire in the shed and the fire in the cottage. In both cases petrol had been used. It was a fairly obvious conclusion, but nothing had been left to chance. Blood stains had been found on a portion of skirting-board near the back door of the cottage. When examined microscopically the white corpuscles were seen to contain small drumstick-shaped marks peculiar to female blood. The decaying corpse in the heather was of the same blood group, AB. The serologist said that the percentage with this group was only about three to four.

Then an expert in odontology displayed a chart of Jocelyn Carne's teeth. It corresponded exactly with the teeth in the skull of the corpse. This was shown to the jury.

Identification having been established, evidence now moved on to the cause of death.

Professor Miles Benford took the stand. Work in a forensic laboratory is to most pathologists a means of livelihood, but for Benford it was a great deal more. He was an admirer of Professor Mikhail Gerasimov, the Russian forensic expert in facial reconstruction who had set up the Laboratory for Plastic Reconstruction in the Ethnographical Institute of the USSR Academy of Sciences. Gerasimov had died in 1970. Benford's own work in the same field had over the years acquired a degree of competence almost equal to the master's. He only wished Gerasimov could have seen it.

The judge, aware of what he was like as an expert witness, sat back grimly and awaited the inevitable.

Breddon asked Benford to tell the jury his qualifications, which were impressive, and then he moved on smoothly to the murder.

'Would you tell us, Professor, how Jocelyn Carne came to die?'

Benford would, with much enthusiasm. His voice was high-pitched and he talked very fast. He used his pink chubby hands a lot, bringing them together as if he were squeezing something between them and then flinging them apart again. He smiled frequently, his eyes crinkling with benevolence. Most people liked him at first sight but began having reservations as they listened to him. He could have given his evidence in a couple of minutes, but chose to prolong it. Jocelyn Carne had been struck about the head several times by a sharp instrument. One of the blows had struck her across the bridge of the nose and broken it. He had brought photographs of her skull which illustrated what he was talking about. For most forensic experts they would have been sufficient.

Spencer-Leigh was a judge of some kindness and he couldn't repress a feeling of sympathy for Carne when he had agreed to Benford's request for the exhibit in the plastic bag to be shown.

Carne, unaware that he was about to see a modelled reconstruction of Jocelyn's head, felt as shocked as if a knife had ripped his stomach when Benford removed the model from its wrappings. He bent forward over his folded arms, holding in the pain, forcing himself to remain silent. It was the only emotion he had shown since the trial started. The audience in the public gallery watched him curiously. McNair turned and looked at him too. He had tried to stop this exhibit before coming into court, but had been overruled. Benford, according to Breddon, needed it to show the extent of the wounding. 'And even more importantly,' Spencer-Leigh had said drily, 'his wonderful artistry, given a death mask and a few hairs.'

The reconstruction was brilliant. Jocelyn Carne hadn't been a pretty woman, but she'd had a certain homely charm. The face was small and oval-shaped, the nose stubby like her daughter's. The area of the nasal fracture was shown by a small thread-like line.

Benford pointed to it. 'It seems likely that the first blow landed here. She could have been lying in a bed or reclining in a chair. The fact that the blood stains were found near the back door doesn't necessarily mean that the murder took place there. It could have happened in the bedroom or the sitting-room. Those areas were completely gutted. Most of the bleeding occurred when the blows fractured her skull.'

He moved his hands through the model's thick, short, dark hair, almost lovingly, before removing the wig.

'Heavy blows to the skull vault sent multiple fissures from the main site.' He had drawn these with a deep plum-coloured pigment. 'Here you'll see the main fissure—the principal line of force. I didn't obscure the pattern of the blows with blood. There would have been a lot of blood.' He picked up a life-sized diagram and put it next to the head. 'This is a coronal section through the vault of the head showing the relation of the skull to the cerebral vein and the meningeal artery and vein.'

He turned to the judge. 'I should like the jury, my Lord, to see these at close quarters.'

Spencer-Leigh asked if that was necessary.

'With respect, my Lord, I think it is.'

The judge nodded. 'Very well, if you must.' He watched the usher carrying the head and the diagram over to the jury. If he were a betting man he would have laid the odds on the nervous young woman, Trina Thompson, passing out first. He would have lost his money. He saw with some astonishment that it was the mature, seemingly self-possessed Selina McKay who was staggering to her feet, her handkerchief pressed to her lips.

Selina managed to reach the door before the floor, black and hot, rushed up and sucked her into it. She came to after several minutes to find that she was being tended by a sympathetic policewoman. Later, when the bones in her legs became solid again, the policewoman took her gently by the arm and led her to the washroom. 'Bathe your face with cold water,' she advised, 'and put a damp paper towel on the back of your neck.'

Selina apologised. 'It was dreadful of me to make such a fool of myself.'

The policewoman told her to think nothing of it. 'If it hadn't been you, it would have been someone else. Benford's exhibits are usually gruesome. The judge will have ordered coffee for just about now, so there'll be a recess for about half an hour.' She went over to the washroom door and stood aside as Elaine Balfour came in. 'Here's one of your friends coming to see if you're okay.'

Elaine Balfour was a woman of considerable tact. 'To speed my own recovery with a glass of water,' she said briskly, 'failing some medicinal brandy.'

She waited until the policewoman had gone out before saying what she thought of Benford.

'Dreadful man—appalling wax-work—how dare he thrust it at us like that!'

She looked closely at Selina. 'Feeling better?'

'I think so.' But she was terrified of doing it again. Terrified of going back in.

Selina wet some paper towels and did as the policewoman had suggested. Her hair was damp and straggling and fell in wisps to her shoulders. She tried to tidy it.

'When I was a young woman,' Elaine told her, 'I married a farmer. In those days one pig was regularly killed for family use. I was a Londoner, not used to that sort of thing. When I saw my first dead pig, slain by my otherwise civilised husband, I was both sick and outraged. Carne's idyllic versions of farm life make me squirm; his violence is something else again. There aren't any words for it.'

'If he did it,' Selina said.

'Quite.' Elaine poured herself a glass of water and sipped it slowly. 'I'm impressionable. I jump to conclusions, and then I change my mind. Not good jury material, perhaps, but it's not my fault. I didn't ask to be called.'

She drank the water, then rummaged in her handbag and took out a pair of ear-plugs wrapped in cellophane. 'I even brought these. Just in case I couldn't stand it. I think your need is greater than mine. They're sterile. Never used. Would you like them?'

She put the ear-plugs on the edge of the

washbasin. Selina eyed them with guilty longing. 'But we're supposed to listen to the evidence. I've sworn an oath. We've a duty to Carne. I can't possibly...'

'If that monster in the dock wreaked that sort of havoc on his wife's head,' Elaine exclaimed, 'a little intermittent deafness shouldn't trouble your conscience. If you sit next to me you can put them in when you want to and I'll prod you when it's safe to take them out again.'

Ashamed but grateful, Selina accepted them.

★ ★ ★

When the judge returned to the court twenty minutes later he said graciously that he hoped Mrs McKay was feeling better. Selina, not hearing him, gazed blankly in front of her. Spencer-Leigh, believing her to be still in a state of shock, shrugged and hoped for the best. Benford, as far as he knew, had done his worst.

With the new seating arrangement, Selina was in the front row next to Elaine and in front of Quinn. Quinn, looking at her intently, saw the ear-plugs. So much for British justice and the jury system, he thought. He couldn't blame her. He was in no position to blame anyone. The head had been uncannily like Frances's head. It would be difficult to rub the image out of his mind when he saw her again. The strength of his emotional involvement was just becoming apparent to him. When he saw the battered scalp after the wig had been removed he had wanted to go over to Carne and kill him. As bloodily as possible. In that shocking moment murdered Jocelyn had become murdered Frances. It had taken him a little while to separate the two and calm himself. Now, slowly becoming more rational, more objective, he allowed the necessary element of doubt back into his mind. It was impossible for him not to be influenced by Frances, but if doubt could be nurtured, then any harm he might do Carne would be held in check. He looked across the courtroom at Carne. His face was grey as if it had been wiped over with a dirty rag. His eyes were half-closed. Frances's father. No physical resemblance. She tore up your newspaper photograph. I burnt it. That's what you are to her—ash in my living-room grate. And what is she to you? Do you ever wonder where the hell she is? Have you any compassion for her at all?

Carne's thoughts of Frances were deliberately set nine years in the past. He remembered it as a tranquil period. She was ten years old. He was walking along the Bristol docks with her, and her hand in his was warm, dry and comforting. The waves were lapping against the boats. It was a clean sound. The air smelt of salt. He focused on her hand in his and refused to think of anything else. The rest of the evidence that Benford was giving was like the low muttering of a sinister wind. He closed his ears to it and refused to let the sound become words.

At the end of Benford's evidence, McNair briefly cross-examined.

'Blood stains were found near the back door,' he said. 'You stated that Jocelyn Carne was probably recumbent at the time of the attack— in bed—or on a chair. Is it feasible that she was neither sitting down, nor lying down? That she had, in fact, been knocked down?'

'It's possible—yes. It can't be proved either way. If she *was* pushed down, no bones were broken.'

'If it can't be proved, then it can't be disproved. She could have gone to answer a knock at the back door—or she could have heard her assailant forcing an entry that way. Entry by any of the cottage windows would have been impossible; they were small and latticed. Her confrontation with her killer could have taken place there, where the blood stains were found. Murder committed in the course of burglary, perhaps.'

Benford shrugged. It was his job to provide forensic evidence, not to assist defence counsel with his conjectures.

McNair had made his point and didn't enlarge on it. With a weak defence it was necessary to widen the field. A non-domestic murder committed by person or persons unknown might be hard to believe, but unless he could come up with something better it would have to do.

Before telling Benford he could stand down, the judge had a question for him. 'The accused, Edward Carne, was unable to identify his wife. Was this a refusal to identify her, or genuine inability?'

'The body was in an advanced state of decomposition,' Benford pointed out. 'Extreme disfiguration occurs in a matter of weeks. The body had been lying in the ground for several months. The cold weather during the winter would have retarded the process only very slightly. After the first month there would be general liquefaction and disruption of the soft tissues. Between four and five months there would be adipocere of face, head and breasts, followed by adipocere of arms, legs and internal organs.'

He was about to go on, but Spencer-Leigh stopped him. 'I have a great regard for your knowledge, Professor Benford, but the jury and I are amateurs in these matters. We don't need to know the medical details. Would Edward Carne have recognised his wife?'

'Psychologically there would be a deep aversion to looking at her.'

'But would he have known her?'

'No, my Lord, without remnants of clothing to help him, he would not.'

'The corpse was buried fully dressed,'

Spencer-Leigh said. 'He had more than remnants of clothing to go on.'

'Then I can't answer you. I don't know his state of mind. There could have been strong revulsion. The general condition of the body would have affected the clothing.' He smiled. 'Do you wish me to elaborate?'

Spencer-Leigh didn't. 'I take your point.'

CHAPTER FIVE

Lunch was eaten without enthusiasm by the majority of the jury. Selina skipped it altogether and went for a walk in the fresh air. Quinn went back to the restaurant he had gone to the previous day and was joined there by Peter Lomax, the carpet salesman. For Lomax the horrors of the morning had merged in his mind with the horrors perpetrated by the Middle Eastern revolutionaries. He told Quinn about the difficulties encountered by the carpet trade. War had affected traditional markets. Buyers had to go further afield. China was stable. The prices there were high, but you were paying for quality. Next year he hoped to go to Peking. His carpet-buying trip this year had been cancelled because of the trial.

Quinn sympathised and said drily that it was unfortunate that both the mullahs and Carne were so disruptive.

Lomax, unsure whether to take it as a joke or as sarcasm, looked at him sharply. 'It isn't pleasant. Not any of it. I'm happily married. It's quite beyond my comprehension that anyone, especially a smoothie like Carne, could have...' He stopped abruptly and looked about him. This was a public place. He lowered his voice. 'I don't suppose we should be talking about it. There's still a long way to go. But it's difficult just to stick with generalities. My wife's one of his fans. She'd arrange an early evening meal the nights he was on the box so that she could settle back afterwards and watch his programme. She said he was ... civilised.' She had said it the night a seed from a blackberry tart had lodged under Lomax's denture. No seed, she had implied, would have lodged under Carne's denture—not that he wore dentures— but if he did, and if one had, he would retire in a civilised manner to the bathroom to remove it. The criticism still made him hot with annoyance. Quinn's expression didn't calm him. 'I'm sorry,' he said stiffly, 'if I've been boring you.'

'You haven't,' Quinn lied politely.

*   *   *

During the afternoon, the prosecuting counsel, having established death by murder, began constructing sufficient circumstantial evidence to justify Carne's presence in the dock.

Breddon's first witness was one of the forensic team who had been working in the grounds of the cottage following the fire. The lane up to the cottage had shown the imprint of several superimposed tyre marks. In the immediate vicinity of the cottage there was a tarmacked area where cars could be parked. Before entering the tarmacked area there was a field off to the left. Here there was clear evidence of the deeply imprinted tyre marks of one car. Whoever had driven his car up there had probably done so before setting the cottage alight.

'Have you any idea why the car had been driven such a distance from the cottage?' Breddon asked.

'To be a safe distance from the blaze,' Inspector Thompson answered. 'If the fire hadn't been planned the car would have been left on the tarmacked area and the petrol tank would have ignited.'

He had gone on to explain that the cars of suspected arsonists had had their tyres checked against the prints of the car. 'Nothing matched. One of the tyres of the car in the field had trapped a piece of metal. The tyre was an ordinary commercial brand used by thousands of motorists—the trapping of the metal made it uniquely distinctive. It might have penetrated.

Hard to say. It could have caused a slow puncture. It showed up quite clearly on the prints.'

'Would it have been helpful in tracing the car?'

'Most certainly.'

'What kind of car was it?' Breddon wanted to know. 'A mini—something larger—a station wagon, perhaps?'

'A car of medium weight. Probably a family saloon. The field was muddy. It went into a spin when reversing out. Something had been put under the back wheels to give it grip. Whatever it was, the driver removed it. This shows up as a smudged area on the photographs.'

'Could you find any other evidence of the driver's presence?' asked Breddon.

'Apart from the tyre marks, none,' Thompson answered.

Breddon asked permission for photographs of the tyre imprints to be handed to the jury. After the traumatic photographs of the morning they were looked at with some relief.

McNair did not bother to cross-examine.

The next witness Breddon called was a Mr Weston, the owner of a small garage in the hamlet of Long Acre on the A5 less than one hour's drive from the cottage. Weston hoped the publicity of the trial would help business and he gave his evidence with a degree of confidence.

Breddon asked him if he recognised the

prisoner in the dock.

'Yes, sir. That's Edward Carne. He called at my garage on the morning of the fourth of August.'

'At what time was this?'

'Shortly after seven. He needed petrol.'

'What make of car was he driving?'

'A Ford Granada. Very muddy. I suggested he might like to put it through the car-wash. He said he was in a hurry and then he changed his mind. He asked me to put it through for him. While the car was being washed he went into the shop to pay. He gave my assistant cash for the petrol and then he noticed we had a special offer on tyres. They could have been bought singly, but he decided to buy the four. By this time the car had been washed and I took over the sale of the tyres.'

'How did he pay you for the tyres?'

'By credit card. I asked him if he wished my mechanic to replace any of the tyres on his car. He said he didn't, but he recognised a bargain when he saw one. He told the mechanic to put two in the boot and two on the back seat.'

'Was there luggage in the boot?'

'There was a small suitcase and a bundle of something covered with sacking. The sacking was muddy. It must have been a big bundle because there was only room enough for the two tyres.'

'Did you notice if the tyres on the Granada

were the same make as the ones you sold him?'

Weston said they weren't and mentioned the make. 'They were in good condition. Almost new. But one needed air. I told him this. He said he hadn't time to bother. I got the impression that he wanted to get back to London rather quickly.'

McNair half-rose to his feet. Breddon, anticipating the objection, asked if Carne had mentioned London to him.

'No, I don't think so. I'm not sure.'

'Try to keep your evidence factual,' Breddon warned him. 'Would you say the tyre that needed air had a slow puncture?'

'It's likely. I didn't get close enough to look. If it had, then I suppose he put his spare on further along.'

McNair's cross-examination was brief. 'The defendant paid you by credit card for the tyres, that is not disputed. That he was at your garage on the date in question is not disputed. He bought four new tyres because he knew a bargain when he saw one. Very sensible of him. You have a good memory, Mr Weston?'

Weston nodded, 'I suppose so—yes.'

'On the morning of the fourth of August did you put many cars through the car-wash?'

'Probably. I remember putting the Granada through.'

'But you have no distinct recollection of any of the other cars?'

67

'No, it would be impossible to . . .'

'To remember after such a lapse of time? I agree. But you remember the Granada, and that it was muddy. You remember that there was a small suitcase in the boot—and a bundle of something covered with sacking. Interesting. You also noticed that one of the tyres was flat. You seem to be gifted with almost total recall in this one instance.'

'Edward Carne wasn't just any Tom, Dick or Harry of a customer,' Weston said with some acerbity. 'It's natural for him to stick in my mind.'

'Natural, too, to read about him in the tabloids.' McNair picked up a sheaf of newspaper articles from the table. 'Most of these comment on the defendant's life-style—his house—his hobbies—the make of his car. They were all published recently when interest in the case began to be aroused.'

'I don't need a newspaper to tell me he drove a Granada,' Weston protested.

'I'm sure you don't,' McNair agreed. 'By the way, what colour was it?'

Weston hesitated. 'Blue.'

'Not a lucky guess,' McNair said. He ran his fingers along the edge of the cuttings and then put them back on the table. 'The gentlemen of the press weren't colour-conscious either. None of them mentioned it. For your information, the car was brown.' He smiled pleasantly at

68

Weston. 'I'm not suggesting that you have been deliberately misleading in your evidence, but I do suggest that your imagination has been at work here and there, influenced possibly by what you've read.' He turned to Spencer-Leigh, 'I have no more questions for this witness, my Lord.'

The evidence during the rest of the afternoon followed a similar pattern. The proprietor of Carne's London garage produced invoices to show that Carne's tyres had been bought in July. So why, Breddon asked, buy new ones at the Long Acre garage in August? They hadn't been all that cheap. And why go to the bother of changing them himself when his own garage would have done it for him—had it been necessary?

The last witness, Reginald Markham, was a member of the Round Table. His twelve-year-old son had gone around the district asking for anything combustible for Bonfire Night. Carne had given him two tyres. It had seemed a shame to burn them, Markham had said, as they were in very good nick. He had been tempted to keep them for himself, but had resisted the temptation.

'Commendably honest of you,' Breddon said, 'but in the circumstances unfortunate. Two tyres disposed of on a bonfire. Two others untraceable, but most certainly disposed of as well.' He let his glance linger on the jury and then spoke with quiet emphasis, 'I wonder why?'

The jury, by this time, felt that the point was being laboured rather too hard. They could sum up the evidence of the day in three sentences. Jocelyn Carne had been murdered. Her husband had been within easy driving distance of the cottage early the following morning. He had behaved suspiciously by getting rid of four good tyres. All this, they believed, could have been put across with far less trauma and a good deal less repetition. When the court rose they were all ready to go home.

Quinn bought copies of all the evening newspapers in the hope that one of them could be passed to Frances without causing her too much damage. After skimming through them in the car park he decided that none of them could, and put them in the rubbish container. He realised that the buskers might bring a newspaper back, but then if they did the poison wouldn't have been administered by him. Not that they would push anything unpleasant at her with deliberate intent. So far, they had been very protective of her. Though only a few years older they were treating her like an ill child. Evidence of their care was shown differently depending on their personalities. Stu, a Canadian, the only professionally trained musician in the group, made dry, nervous, little speeches to her on any innocuous subject that came into his mind. Lucille, a volatile hybrid, part Cockney, part French, bought her necessities such as tampons and a toothbrush and lent her clothes. Nils showed her how to strum his guitar and was pleased when for a few brief minutes she appeared to show interest in it. Blossom cooked for her and extolled the virtues of milk when she thought Frances was drinking too much, which was most of the time. It worried Quinn that she was fast becoming a lush, but unlike Blossom he was careful not to show it. He supposed she needed the booze to cope.

As soon as he got home he went searching for her. She wasn't in any of the downstairs rooms and he asked Blossom where she was. Blossom was ironing Stu's shirt in the kitchen. Her exquisite little face under its piled-up glossy hair showed signs of strain. 'In the bedroom. She's been there all day, I think.' She added that Frances had taken down the poster of Snoopy. 'She said she couldn't stand it.'

The Snoopy poster, the last reminder of Timothy's occupancy, had been sellotaped over the dressing-table. A swaggering dog, Quinn realised, wasn't soothing. He didn't mind her taking it down. When Timothy slept there again—on a brief visit—he would have developed other interests. And the gap between them would have widened even more. He retreated hastily from his own problems and

71

asked if Frances had eaten.

Blossom said she had left her a salad on a tray and a glass of milk. She didn't tell Quinn about the half-bottle of gin she had removed from Frances's room or that Frances had followed her down to the kitchen and demanded it back. In the ensuing altercation Blossom had refused to be drawn into a full-scale row. 'Drink,' she told her, 'solves nothing.' She had placed a sisterly arm around her shoulders and called her Frankie. Frances, shaking with barely controlled rage, had pushed her away and taken the gin bottle. 'My name,' she said, 'is Frances—not your godawful diminutive—and who's trying to solve anything? Who the hell can?'

Blossom unplugged the iron. 'I'm very worried about her. She needs comforting, Robert. Proper comforting. Getting pissed is no good.'

Blossom's occasional lapses into the vocabulary of the other buskers always took Quinn by surprise. It was like scrawling graffiti across the Hall of Supreme Harmony. Her use of the word 'comfort' translated simply to 'sex'. She comforted Stu most nights. Frequently she comforted him. On the nights she was available she would leave her herb pillow on his bed an hour or so before she appeared—to be returned, she hinted delicately, if he had other plans. Who, he wondered, did Blossom have in mind to comfort Frances? Stu? Nils? Himself? Or had she meant the word in its more usual sense? He looked at her, puzzled.

She picked up Stu's shirt and began folding it. It smelt warm and looked cared for. A domesticated environment could be comfortable when presided over by a beautiful Chinese. He wondered how he'd feel if some time in the future the other buskers went on their way and left her behind? Burdened? Pleased? Comforted?

'To comfort Frances,' he told her, 'in any sense of the word, can only be done when she's ready for it. Just feed her. Put up with her. Don't smother her with concern. And, whatever you do, keep today's papers from her.'

While the buskers were out on their nightly stint he spent an hour cosseting his orchids. The wine-red Vuylstekeara Cambria Flush had lost some of its heads and so had the rose and purple Dendrobium Phalaenopsis. He hoped they had fallen naturally, thinking of the orchid Frances was wearing last night. To put an orchid in the waistband of her skirt had been a good sign. The patient was rallying. Today, there was a relapse. He knew from his own, much milder experiences, that depression was a black quicksand; the more you struggled, the more it sucked you down. In the end you survived because you kidded yourself you were okay. He was okay now. The buskers had walked in on his solitude and made friendly noises. They had come along at the right time. Frances hadn't. She had dropped a rock in the pool of his content and stirred up feelings of compassion, of anxiety.

Before going to bed he knocked at her door. She didn't answer. He knocked again. 'I only need to know,' he said, 'that you're all right.'

She assured him, after a few minutes' pause, that she was. 'It's just that I can't sleep.'

Neither could he. The street lamp shone through the open slats of the Venetian blinds and threw bar-like shadows over the walls of his bedroom. He kept thinking of Carne—of Jocelyn—of their daughter in the small bedroom down the corridor. Shortly after one, he heard her going downstairs. When she hadn't returned after half an hour he put on his towelling robe and went down to join her.

She had been searching in the living-room and the kitchen for the day's papers and, after her first startled glance at him, told him so. 'You brought them home last night. You must have brought them home tonight, too. I've got to see them.'

He told her that he hadn't. 'I'm going to heat up some coffee. Will you have some?'

'Were they too bad for you to bring?'

'No,' he lied, 'there was just too much of a queue at the kiosk.'

She was shivering in a short blue cotton

74

nightdress, which was too tight across the rump. Probably one of Lucille's. He switched on the electric heater. 'Nils's jacket is on the back of the door. Wrap it around you.'

She was a replica of her mother and he couldn't get the resemblance out of his head. If she were completely in purdah he could speak to her better.

She sensed his discomfort and misinterpreted it. 'Do you want me to get dressed?'

'No—but I want you to be warm.'

Nil's coat was long, shaggy and dirty. She grimaced with distaste before putting it around her shoulders.

It was unwise, perhaps, but he made the coffee Irish.

She told him that she had been listening to the radio account of the trial. 'It was a very short account, but it mentioned a professor. And he brought in a . . .' She couldn't say it.

He said it for her, sensing that it was better spoken about. 'It was a model. An unnecessary piece of egotistical display. The photographs were sufficient. It shouldn't have been allowed.'

'How did my father react?' Her eyes, dark like her mother's, were watching him intently.

He told her the truth. 'It upset him, but only for a moment or two. He's always been in full control of himself.'

He waited for her to say more and after a while she did. Her approach was oblique. 'That

75

Snoopy poster belonged to your son?'

'Yes.'

'You miss him?'

'Sometimes.'

'Do you hate your wife?'

'She isn't my wife any longer and I don't hate her.' He supposed he would have to bear with the inquisition if it led somewhere.

'When you were married to her, did you sleep around?'

'Now and then.'

'Did she mind?'

'It never occurred to me to ask her.'

'Did she know?'

'I hope not.'

She nodded her head slowly. 'That's the difference.'

He tried to work it out. The difference between him and her father? Carne's relationships were public. Everyone knew about them. He wondered at what age Frances had become aware of sex, and more specifically, of her father's infidelities. Had her mother thrown jealous tantrums? Had the house reverberated with sexual storms? Was that the basis of her hate? Had she walked in on her father when he was making love to one of his mistresses?

He asked if her father's extra-marital relationships had upset her mother. It sounded stiff, like the jargon of the courts.

'You could say that.'

He would prefer her to say it—clearly. It was necessary to understand. 'What do you mean?'

'He crippled her.'

It was an odd, over-emotional word. 'You were very fond of her?'

She finished her coffee and then took the bottle from the table and half-filled her cup with neat whisky. He regretted leaving it in view, but resisted the urge to take it from her.

'She was my mother,' she said simply. 'I didn't like what my father was doing to her.'

He asked why her parents hadn't divorced.

'Because my dear daddy didn't want to. It was very convenient for him the way it was.' Her full lips twisted into a grimace. 'I overheard Hester bitching to him about it. "Why stay with that pathetic woman," she said, "when you can be free?"'

'You overheard him and the Allendale woman having a row? Was this just before the cottage was gutted?' He was leaning forward, his voice sharp with interest.

She looked at him, frowning. 'Mr bloody barrister for the prosecution,' she said, swaying. 'I'm a hostile witness—hostile to the whole bloody set-up. Go sod yourself and leave me bloody well alone.'

She walked over to the table and gripped it, her back to him. The coat slipped from her and fell rumpled around her feet. She was breathing deeply, stiff with tension, her head bent. Her

77

short, rough, dark hair was Jocelyn's. Watching her, he saw her mother's scars and sensed her own. He didn't know what to do or say.

When she turned to him tears were running down her cheeks. She poured more whisky into her cup. 'This,' she said gulping it, 'smashes it out of my head for a bit—this way I can bear it.'

She picked up the coat and took it over to the sofa. There she wrapped herself in it and sat half-crouched, her face hidden in the collar so that he couldn't see her tears.

'I was insensitive,' he told her gently. 'I shouldn't have questioned you.'

Her voice was muffled. 'I can never go into the witness-box.'

'No.'

'How long will you let me stay?'

'Until it's over.'

'Until it's over,' she repeated.

The words sounded doom-laden. There was a terrible finality about them. He realised just how frightened she was and didn't know how to console her.

He drew up a chair on the other side of the fireplace and watched her covertly. The empty cup of whisky was on the floor beside her. She was no longer crying. Her forehead was mottled with heat. He switched off the electric fire. They sat in silence for a long time and then, when he thought she was verging on sleep, she pulled the collar of the coat away from her face and began speaking about her mother. Her voice was slurred and she spoke in short, fragmented sentences, more to herself than to him. It was a eulogy tinged with desperation; a re-creation of the dead into impossible perfection. Mummy was the one, good, wonderful parent. Daddy she didn't mention at all.

CHAPTER SIX

Edward Carne's housekeeper was giving evidence. He had thought she liked him, evidently she didn't. He folded his arms and listened with amused detachment to what she had to say. She was wearing a blue and white dress and jacket that Jocelyn had given her last summer. Jocelyn's figure had begun to thicken during the last few years. She had been ten stone in weight and only five foot four in height. Mrs Hooper apparently didn't mind wearing the cast-offs of a woman who'd been murdered.

Carne's thoughts were bobbing around like a stringless kite in a high wind. Lack of sleep had made him light-headed. The prison doctor had given him sleeping tablets but he had hidden them in a slit in the mattress. He had a cell to himself and that was supposed to be lucky in these days of overcrowding. It *was* lucky.

Privileged. Like having that bridal suite in the hotel in Buxton because a wedding had been cancelled. The television programme had been about well-dressing in Derbyshire. He had discussed the pagan origins of it with the prison padre who had sat with him for a little while yesterday after he had been brought back from the court. *Arcadia* was an innocuous topic. 'An excellent series,' the padre had enthused, 'the modern man's Eden.' One Adam, he'd thought, too many Eves. The joke had almost been spoken. Perhaps he had said it. He couldn't remember. The padre had pressed his shoulder encouragingly. 'Chin up,' he'd said, like a jolly sportsmaster, 'chin up!' If you put your chin up, an arrogant tilting of the jaw, it was an invitation to violence. The crowds in the street were violent. Or they would be, given the chance. Still some cheers, though. Still some clapping. Well done, Carne, you're giving your usual smooth performance. The padre wanted to know if he could do anything for him. 'Shrive me, Father, for I have sinned.' He actually said it. His brain produced mocking remarks and they fell off his tongue before he could stop them. He'd apologised. The padre had been puzzled by the apology. He'd taken him seriously—obviously hoping for a confession. After that, he'd looked at him oddly. What sort of code of behaviour was expected of him? The prison psychiatrist had asked some fairly obvious questions at the commencement of the trial. Nobody, since the trial began, was subtle. Professor Benford hadn't been subtle yesterday. He hadn't taken the tablets because he was afraid he might dream of Jocelyn headless. Dreams were treacherous. Before leaving, the padre had asked him if he wanted to pray. No, he'd told him. God, if there was a God, knew all about it. Not the padre. Not this circus in here. Certainly not Mrs Hooper who was doing a good job of character assassination. She was telling the prosecuting counsel that he used to bring his women home. As if he bedded them in pairs. She was probably referring to Joanna and Clare who were working on the scripts. They'd come a couple of times when Jocelyn was away. If mud flew in their direction it would be unfortunate— and unfair. It had been a working relationship and nothing more. He supposed he'd better tell McNair.

He tried to attract his attention and eventually succeeded. McNair told him not to worry. He wasn't worrying. He wished he were. It would be normal, but then he hadn't felt normal since Benford had shocked him yesterday.

After a few minutes McNair began batting on his side. Considering he'd only just been told about the scriptwriters, he managed to put the point over very well. Whether the jury believed him or not was another matter.

'You have already told my learned friend the

nature of your duties,' he said. 'You clean. You cook. You shop. Did you at any time assist Mr Carne with his broadcasting work?'

She was surprised. 'Certainly not. I'm not qualified.'

'You are aware that the programmes are rehearsed to the last detail?'

She shrugged. 'Yes, I suppose so.'

'Would you be able to differentiate between Mr Carne's working colleagues and his family friends?'

'I knew Mrs Carne's friends. They were nice respectable ladies.'

'Nice respectable ladies also exist outside the circle of Mrs Carne's friends. Isn't it likely that Mr Carne would sometimes invite his working colleagues home so that they might work late on a script?'

'It's funny they should do it when Mrs Carne wasn't there.'

McNair looked surprised. 'You're telling me that Mrs Carne was one of a working team? That she assisted her husband and his colleagues with the programmes?'

'She had nothing to do with them.'

'Then why should you comment on her absence? Why was it funny, as you put it, that they should occasionally come in her absence?'

Mrs Hooper was getting flustered. 'You know quite well what I mean.'

Spencer-Leigh intervened. 'I suggest you get

back to the original line of questioning, Mr McNair. According to my notes, Mrs Hooper was out shopping when the defendant returned on the morning of August the fourth. She was under the impression that he had driven up from his television job in Devon. His comings and goings didn't follow a fixed routine and he frequently forgot to inform her about them. Neither did he inform her when he would be returning with guests. Mrs Hooper's interpretation of the word "guests" caused the deviation which occurred at that point.'

'My Lord, I must respectfully remind you that my learned friend, Mr Breddon, must have been aware of the deviation and did nothing to stop it.'

'Nevertheless,' the judge said firmly, 'I am stopping it now. Have you anything to ask this witness that relates to that particular very crucial day? If you have, then please get on with it.'

McNair inclined his head politely. 'My Lord.' He turned back to Mrs Hooper. 'When Mr Carne had the telephone call about the fire in the cottage and told you what had happened, were you worried about Mrs Carne's safety?'

'No. The police told him there was no one in the cottage. I thought she might have gone visiting friends, or her daughter, perhaps. Frances had a holiday job in Liverpool. And he seemed so cool about it all.' Mrs Hooper smoothed the left cuff of Jocelyn's jacket with the index finger of her right hand. 'But had I known then what I know now...' Her face flushed with genuine emotion and she couldn't go on.

'And had Mr Carne known the full facts then,' McNair stated, 'he would have been deeply shocked, as indeed he was several months later when her body was found.'

He went on quickly before Mrs Hooper's obvious scepticism was vocalised. 'When did he drive to Wales?'

'The next morning.'

'Did he make any special preparation for the journey—such as changing the tyres of his car?'

Mrs Hooper was predictably surprised. 'Good gracious, no! He might have put water in the radiator. I didn't notice.'

'After receiving the telephone call, how did he spend the rest of the day?'

'In his study. Probably seeing to the insurance papers.'

'Did he go into the garden—do a bit of tidying up—burn rubbish, perhaps?'

Completely mystified by the seeming irrelevancy of the questions, Mrs Hooper shook her head. 'He hated gardening. Mrs Carne did it when she was there. He never did anything to help her.'

'Are there open fireplaces in the house?'

'No, they've been boarded up. Mrs Carne

used to put plants in the hearths. The house was pretty when she was there, she . . .'

He interrupted her. 'What sort of central heating is there?'

'Gas.'

'So nothing could be burnt indoors?'

'No.'

'Thank you,' said McNair. 'You've been very helpful.'

He glanced at Carne before sitting down. Carne would, of course, have changed the tyres when Mrs Hooper wasn't around and if he had blood-stained clothing he was hardly likely to burn it in his own garden. He had probably done all the burning at the cottage and then changed into clean clothes before driving home. It was difficult to conduct a defence when you were ninety-per-cent sure that the defendant was guilty. It didn't bother his conscience, but it stretched his professional competence like a piece of frayed string. Carne's stubborn refusal, or inability, to produce an alibi for the night of the third of August made his task almost impossible. He couldn't put him in the witness-box. Breddon would demolish him.

Carne's television producer was the next witness. He and his team had been setting up a programme about the Doone Valley, he told Breddon. Carne had asked permission to leave before the programme was completed. As Carne was a dedicated professional, he knew that he must have had an urgent reason for going, though Carne didn't offer any explanation. His sudden departure was awkward, but it was possible to complete the local filming without him and do the rest in the London studio. This they did, after a lapse of a few days.

Breddon confirmed with the producer that the hurried departure of Carne from the set had occurred on the morning of the third of August and noted out loud that on the following morning, the fourth of August, at around seven o'clock he was within an hour's drive of the gutted cottage and on his way back to London.

Before the producer left the stand, Breddon asked him if it was usual for the scriptwriters to work with Carne in his own home. The producer, who hadn't heard the earlier evidence, said it wasn't. They might visit socially, of course. Breddon couldn't resist a smile in McNair's direction. McNair ignored it. He didn't bother trying to resurrect that particular barricade. Oddly, though, he sensed that in that one particular Carne had been telling him the truth.

Olivia Mason, a striking-looking woman in her thirties, followed the producer into the witness-box. She wore her black hair in a thick plait down her back and was dressed in a fawn coloured skirt and jacket, woven in her craft centre in Snowdonia. Her heavily lidded dark brown eyes were carefully averted from Carne.

Carne, troubled for the first time that morning by a sense of reality, leaned forward and watched her intently for a moment or two before looking away. He glanced at the jury without seeing any individual. They were an amorphous mass of faces. His eyes focused momentarily on Quinn and then moved on.

Quinn, aware of Carne's reaction, became alert. Between Carne and this witness there was a bond. Had dear Daddy been dallying with her, too?

Breddon, after the usual preliminaries, asked her about the location of her home. She told him that the craft centre and adjoining cottage where she lived were about a couple of miles from the village of Brynglas.

'And the Carnes' cottage—where was that in relation to the craft centre?'

'A mile across the fields—a little further by road.' Her voice was rich and deep with just the slightest intonation of a Welsh accent.

'Did you know the Carnes?'

'Yes. When they bought the cottage they furnished it with a few hand-made items from the craft centre. My husband was a carpenter. He made Welsh dressers in pine. I did the weaving. Jocelyn Carne bought some of my tweed curtain material.'

'So you knew them as customers. Did you know them socially?'

'We met occasionally. They had supper with

us once or twice.'

'Would you regard them as a happy couple?'

'They behaved well towards each other.'

Breddon pursed his lips. 'Is that your definition of being happy—a polite regard for each other?'

She looked at him coolly. 'I saw nothing in their behaviour to suggest they might not be happy.'

'They never quarrelled in your presence?'

'No.'

'Perhaps you didn't see them—as a couple— sufficiently often to be able to form an opinion of them?'

'Possibly. Jocelyn spent a lot of time on her own in the cottage. She was a strong and self-sufficient woman. It wasn't in her nature to be lonely. She loved the country and liked to go walking.'

'On her own?'

'Yes, why not?'

'Did her daughter visit her at the cottage?'

'Yes. She was studying at one of the northern universities. She drove down in her mini occasionally.'

'Did you meet her?'

'Once, very briefly, in the village. She was gauche—rather shy. Jocelyn was obviously very fond of her.'

'So the mother-daughter relationship was a warm one.' Breddon changed direction. 'How would you describe your husband's relationship with Mrs Carne?'

She looked startled and then amused. 'My husband's...? You're not surely suggesting...?'

'I'm not suggesting anything, merely enquiring. You and your husband were the only villagers who had any social contact with the Carnes. I'm trying to fill in the background to the case.'

She accepted the explanation. 'My husband and I were their neighbours in the usual way. Once or twice my husband helped her out. The back door had become swollen by damp once and he went over and planed it for her—that sort of thing.' She added, 'You know, I suppose, that my husband suffered from cardiac trouble and that he died of a heart attack this January?'

Yes, Breddon said, he knew. He added he was sorry.

He could have spared her the next question, but didn't. 'According to a witness, your husband and Jocelyn Carne were together for about an hour in the local pub a few days before the fire.'

It was her turn to say she knew. 'David had gone down to the village store to get some provisions and had met Jocelyn there. He invited her for a drink. She accepted.'

'I see.'

The innkeeper would tell the court that Jocelyn Carne and David Mason had been arguing quietly but with some vehemence. That was to come later and Breddon didn't intend divulging it just yet.

'Please don't be offended by my next question,' Breddon said politely, 'but was there ever an occasion when your relationship with Edward Carne became more than neighbourly—in a moment of stress, perhaps, would he have gone to you?'

'I hardly ever saw him,' she answered, her colour rising, 'certainly I never saw him on his own. And that's the truth. In a moment of stress? I don't know what you mean. And why come to me?'

She shot Carne a nervous glance. He was sitting as still as a piece of statuary—a study in stone.

'Would it surprise you to know,' Breddon asked, 'that on the night of the fire, a local shepherd saw someone resembling Carne walking along the field path in the vicinity of your craft centre?'

'It would astonish me,' Olivia said brusquely. 'It was a very dark night.'

'Was it?' Breddon asked innocently. 'It's odd you should remember that.' He sat down.

McNair decided not to cross-examine. Olivia Mason had repudiated the suggestion that she might be another of Carne's lovers. If she was a liar she was a good one, despite the unfortunate blush. The possibility that her husband might have been having an affair with Jocelyn might linger in the minds of the jury, but he would only be emphasising it if he brought that up again now. Those two possible motives he would quash in his final speech for the defence—if necessary. It wasn't necessary at this stage.

McNair knew that he would have to discredit the shepherd who was due to be called as soon as Olivia Mason left the witness-box. The judge, however, decided to adjourn for the luncheon recess at that point.

Quinn, in no mood for his company, managed to elude Professor Leary who waved to him in an unusually jocular manner in the main hall, seemingly intent on having a conversation with him. Quinn's lunch consisted of a bar of chocolate eaten in a bookshop. He needed to study a London street map that showed in some detail the best route to Carne's house in Carlisle Crescent. He got the information without buying the map, and instead spent the money on a small second-hand book on Cymbidiums.

When he returned to the jury box the afternoon proceedings were about to begin. Selina McKay turned and smiled at him. It occurred to him that it would have been pleasant to have lunched with her, if he'd had the time. She had stopped wearing the ear-plugs, he noticed, and wondered what she had made of the morning's evidence.

Tom Griffiths, the first witness of the afternoon, was sworn in. He had been a shepherd at one of the hill farms for over twenty years and knew the three hundred acres of rough mountain territory very well. He could walk parts of it in his sleep, he told Breddon, but of course he carried a large heavy-duty torch. He had been attending a ewe that had fallen and broken its leg when he saw Carne on the field path. No, he couldn't be sure of the time—between eleven and midnight was the best he could do. He had left his cottage just after ten-thirty and it was a half-hour's walk. He'd noticed it had gone twelve when he got home—getting on for half-past. He knew it was Carne by his jacket. A yellow and black windcheater with a hood. He'd worn it in the village a few times and looked like a bloody wasp in it.

The judge told him to moderate his language. Griffiths, whose language could be lurid, was surprised the judge was so sensitive. He apologised.

'Are you absolutely sure it was Carne you saw?' Breddon insisted.

'Oh, yes,' said Griffiths. 'No doubt about it at all. He has a peculiar way of walking. It's to do with his shoes.'

'Shoes?'

'Light suede things, not proper country

boots. Brambles attack them. He walked delicately, like going through a mine-field. He was watchful of his feet.'

'I see,' said Breddon and he left it at that.

McNair began his cross-examination. 'Are you often out at night, Mr Griffiths?'

'When needs be. Sheep can get into trouble by night as well as by day.'

'How did you know that the animal, at some late hour before midnight, was in trouble?'

'A hiker had noticed it earlier. He mentioned it down in the village. Someone phoned the farm.'

'A hiker? How was he able to pinpoint the locality?'

'It was near a windbreak of stones close to some druids' stones. A path goes along that way.'

'A favourite walk?' McNair asked.

'Yes, in the summer. Lots of visitors and their bloody dogs.' He looked hastily at the judge. 'Sorry, your honour.'

'And, of course, this was summer,' McNair pointed out. 'Late on the night of the third of August.'

'That's right.'

'It was a dark night, I believe. Do you remember that?'

'Can't say I do,' Griffiths said. 'I had my torch with me. I could see well enough with it.'

'So you saw this man in a distinctive jacket

walking along the field path. How close was he to you?'

'A couple of fields away.'

'Did you greet him? Say "goodnight", or something?'

'No. He wasn't close enough for talk.'

'Was he carrying a torch?'

'Must have been. He'd have tripped over if he hadn't.'

'But you didn't actually see it?'

'No.'

McNair began to speak more sharply. 'Torchlight is very evident on a dark night; clothing is not. Doesn't it seem odd to you that you should notice his jacket—a jacket which was largely black with just some touches of yellow—and not notice the torch?'

Griffiths considered it. 'You expect to see a torch, so you don't think about it. You don't expect to see Mr Carne walking along the field, so that's what you think about. Him and his jacket.'

'You identified him by his jacket—and his suede shoes?'

'I don't know about his shoes that night, but he walked as if he was wearing them.'

'So that leaves us with the jacket.'

'Yes.'

McNair invited him to look up at the public gallery. 'Can you see anyone up there wearing a jacket like Carne's?'

94

Griffiths looked. 'No.'

'Can you see anyone wearing a sports coat like yours?'

Griffiths looked again. 'No.'

'Would you say, then, that your sports coat is unique?'

'It was bought at Marks and Spencers,' Griffiths said. 'I didn't see a single one like Carne's there.'

'Do you believe it was tailored especially for him—this black and yellow very characteristic jacket?'

'I don't know.'

'Of course you do, Mr Griffiths. My client, Mr Carne, wore a wind-cheater, mass-produced like your jacket but by a different firm of clothiers. That particular region of Snowdonia is very popular with hikers. A hiker, by your own admission, reported the injured ewe. I put it to you that you saw someone walking along the field. He was wearing a similar wind-cheater to Carne's—not necessarily the same colour. I doubt you would be able to make out the colour at that distance. You knew that Carne's cottage was in the vicinity so you jumped to the wrong conclusion.'

'Then Mr Evans, the vet, jumped to the wrong conclusion, too,' Griffiths said smugly. 'He was walking right beside me. "What the shit is that television wallah doing out here at this time of night?" he asked me. "Picking bloody buttercups?"'

There was a titter in the public gallery. The judge looked up sharply.

Mr Evans, the vet, had fallen like manna for the sustenance of the prosecuting counsel. He wasn't listed as a witness. Until then nobody had known about him.

McNair, feeling defeated, looked worriedly at Carne. His client's face was expressionless, rigidly controlled. He went on to make his final point. 'I don't doubt that both you and Mr Evans saw someone you thought was Carne,' he said. 'You saw a solitary hiker. One of many solitary hikers who probably passed that way. One of them could have been the murderer of Mrs Carne. She was alone in the cottage and vulnerable. Had you spoken to this hiker, and definitely identified him, your evidence would have been of some value. Under the circumstances, it carries very little weight indeed.'

The next villager to give evidence, Will Hughes, the local baker, claimed to have seen Carne's Granada parked in a layby a couple of miles from the village just as dusk was falling. There was another car parked in front of it. The other car was empty. No, he didn't notice the make. There were two people sitting in the Granada, a woman and Carne. Well ... he thought it was Carne. No, he couldn't be positive. Breddon, hoping for a more emphatic response to his questioning, failed to get it. McNair, relieved to be cross-examining an uncertain witness, reduced his evidence to 'a fanciful web of conjecture'. 'There *may* have been a courting couple in a car, Mr Hughes,' he said, 'and it *may* have been a car similar to the defendant's. As you drove past in your van, your glance was fleeting. Or have you an instinct for voyeurism that prompted you to stop?' The baker hadn't. His glance had, indeed, been very fleeting, he assured McNair. It was just that he had thought it worth mentioning to the police when the enquiries began, otherwise ... McNair cut him off in mid-sentence.

The baker was followed into the witness-box by the inn-keeper who had served Jocelyn Carne and David Mason during lunch-time on Monday, the thirty-first of July. Tom Bowen, short and swarthy, was the conductor of the village choir. He was an articulate and intelligent witness and gave his evidence confidently. David Mason, he told Breddon, was of an excitable temperament. He had noticed that he and Mrs Carne were having a heated discussion about something. He saw with some concern that Mason was getting very red in the face and as he knew he had a heart condition he had gone over to the table on the pretext of removing some empty glasses. The argument had come to a temporary halt, but was resumed when he was out of earshot.

'How long did they stay at the pub—the Crown, isn't it?' Breddon asked.

'No, the Mitre. They were together for about forty minutes. Mrs Carne left first—David stayed for about ten minutes or so after she'd gone.'

'And then . . .?' Breddon prompted.

'And then I noticed Mrs Carne had left her handbag behind. It was on the floor under the table. I took it out to the car park, but she'd gone, so obviously she carried her driving keys separately—or perhaps she'd left them in the car. I gave her an hour to discover her loss and return for it. When she didn't, I phoned her at her cottage. She sounded flustered on the phone. She said there wasn't anything of value in her bag and she didn't want a second trip down to the village in one day. She asked me to keep it for her and she'd be along for it the following day.'

'The following day was Tuesday, the first of August?'

'Correct.'

'Did she call for it?'

'No. I wasn't too happy about having it. She said there was nothing of value in it, but even so . . .' Bowen shrugged. 'You know how it is— a lady's personal possessions—a large heavy handbag stuffed with this and that. And I didn't know Mrs Carne very well—just by sight. The only occasion she had been in my pub was that once with David Mason.'

'So what did you do?'

'I phoned her at her cottage again on Wednesday evening, about seven o'clock. She said she had forgotten about it—that she would be along for it as soon as she could.'

Breddon spoke slowly, emphasising the importance of the question. 'This was the second of August? Wednesday, the second of August?'

'Yes.'

'On the night of the following day, the cottage was set alight after Jocelyn Carne had been very bloodily murdered on the premises.' He waited for the jury to assimilate the fact before going on. 'How did she sound on the phone—normal—apprehensive—?'

'Hard to say. Irritable, perhaps. Annoyed with herself for having forgotten her handbag. It was a nuisance to have to fetch it. She wasn't the sort of woman who liked popping down to the village for a gossip. She wasn't seen around very much.'

'Did the saga of the handbag end there?' Breddon asked.

'No. I happened to mention it to one of my customers. He said he had some eggs to deliver to the riding stables, not far from Mrs Carne's place, and that he'd drive up the track to the Carnes' cottage and give it to her. I couldn't let him do that without phoning Mrs Carne first

99

and telling her. So I phoned her on the morning of Thursday, the third of August.'

'Did she reply?'

Bowen's forehead creased with anxiety. 'I don't know. The phone rang for a long time and then someone picked it up. I said "Is that Mrs Carne?" There was a pause and then the phone was put down. I thought, at first, that she was thoroughly fed up with the fuss I was making about her bag. I was annoyed. I decided not to bother any more—to let her fetch it herself. Had I behaved differently, she might still be alive.'

Breddon told him that he had no cause to reproach himself. 'At what time in the morning was the call made?'

'About eleven.'

'She was probably already dead,' Breddon said, 'but that's something we'll never know.'

He thanked Bowen for giving his evidence so clearly.

Bowen, obviously worried, thanked Breddon for thanking him. He then turned to the judge. 'My Lord, may I have your permission to put something right—to correct a wrong impression?'

Spencer-Leigh, momentarily surprised, said he could.

'All the evidence I have given,' Bowen said, 'is true. David Mason and Mrs Carne were quarrelling—I couldn't help noticing. But I'm quite sure there was never anything wrong

100

between them. What I'm trying to say is that the Masons were a very happily married couple. There was no scandal of any sort. They'd lived in the village for seven years and were well-respected. Mrs Mason is still carrying on her craft business. She's a hard-working widow. During her husband's illness, she nursed him devotedly. I don't want my evidence to cast a slur on them. It wouldn't be right.'

Spencer-Leigh listened without comment. It had been unwise, perhaps, to allow a tender conscience a public salve. He wondered which barrister he'd damaged. Breddon, who was trying to establish a motive—Mason in the marital nest. Or McNair who was desperately searching the hills for a wandering homicidal maniac and needed a more credible candidate. McNair had no desire to cross-examine. To try to hang a murder on Mason would be even more difficult than to conjure up a person or persons unknown.

Carne had listened to Olivia's evidence and the inn-keeper's evidence with deep concentration. It wasn't until Bowen left the witness-box that he realised that his clenched hands had caused some of the fingers to go numb. He rubbed them, and gradually colour and feeling returned. The word 'slur' came into his mind. Odd word to use in a court of law. The place was full of slurs—slurs and calumnies of outrageous fortune. His mind was easing itself free again, latching on to anything that didn't matter. The court was a chimera, best ignored. He wandered from it in his imagination, strolling down acceptably bland pathways where nothing disturbed. Jocelyn, once only, when he wasn't sufficiently alert to stop her, became real for a moment. He blanked her out. He willed himself back to the pre-television days. A domestic background that was mild—dull—safe—not imperilled. But then a word, an accent, perhaps, would change the scene and push him onwards in time. He could smell mountain country, a mixture of heather and gorse and sharp, wet soil. Snowdon brooded in the clouds, reducing the cottage, the whole village, to a handful of rubble.

Someone nudged him. The afternoon proceedings were over. As he got to his feet he became aware of his surroundings again. The jury became individuals once more. He looked at them tiredly and with no resentment. They would think what they were told to think. So let them.

CHAPTER SEVEN

'I hear you let rooms,' Trina Thompson said to Quinn. The jurors had just left the Bailey and he was about to fetch his car when she put a restraining hand on his arm. She was wearing a white blouse and a navy blue pleated skirt. A hat with a badge on it would have completed the picture. A fifth former playing hookey. 'The professor,' she added, 'told me.'

Quinn's astonishment subsided. He guessed that Leary in his own inimitable way was cutting him down to size. A squat had a certain panache. Rooms sounded seedy. He told her gravely that his boarding house was full.

She was disappointed. Her father was taking an interest in the trial and was planning to come up to London, she explained. Her boy-friend had to be got out of her flat before he arrived. All affordable accommodation in London, even the YMCA, was full. She had phoned her friends and her boy-friend had phoned his friends. There was no room anywhere.

Quinn commiserated.

'A sleeping-bag on the floor would do,' she pleaded. 'After all, this trial isn't going to last very long, is it?'

'Possibly not,' Quinn said. 'But my place is over-populated already ... like Brixton,' he added, thinking of Carne.

She told him she had asked some of the other jurors, but without any luck. 'Mr Dalton has a spare room, but he keeps a tank of reptiles in it—as pets!' She shuddered. 'How strange can people be?'

'Quite crazy,' he told her, amused. He

wondered how she would react if he told her he kept Frances. 'A little madness,' he said, 'is no bad thing. Think how dull total sanity would be.'

But madness should have its limits, he reflected as he left her and drove over to Carne's home. Last night Frances had told him that she wanted her mother's photograph—to see her again as she really was. He understood and sympathised. The battered and bloody image had grown in her imagination and needed the antidote of a gentle lady in a silver frame. She hadn't asked him to fetch it, but gave him precise details of its whereabouts—on the bureau, behind the door, in the drawing-room. Anticipating the request he had told her that if anyone went into her home under the present circumstances it would be she and no one else. 'When your mind is clear,' he told her, 'you'll understand that. In the meantime I'll take a drive around and see if you can get in and out again without harassment.'

The house, mellow-bricked and ivy-clad, was at the end of a terrace and faced an enclosed communal garden which was for the use of the local residents. On this pleasant summer evening spiraea glowed crimson and the white blossoms of philadelphus were in full bloom. The area was thick with people and cars. He managed to find a slot for his a couple of blocks away and walked back to the crescent. A police car was parked in front of Carne's wrought-iron gate and there were two police officers sitting in it. There was no vandalism to the front of the property, no daubing on the walls, no breaking of the tall narrow windows. The curtains were drawn downstairs as if it were a house of mourning. A young constable was walking across the lawn towards the back of the house. He carried garden shears. Quinn paused and watched him. A trellised archway divided the back garden from the front and suspended from it was what looked like a bundle of rags, half-burnt. An old television set had been pushed away so that it was to the side of the effigy and was half-hidden by a veronica bush. A placard, scorched and curling at the edges, lay on the grass. The word *carnage* boldly printed across it was still legible. The constable cut down the figure from the cross bar of the trellis. It bore no resemblance to Carne—presumably it once had.

A sudden burst of jungle rhythm from a transistor radio broke the uncanny silence as the crowds watched the policeman with the shears. He moved the effigy with the tip of his shears, and cotton wool, the colour of strong tea, flaked into the air. One of the constables got out of the car by the gate and tried with little success to get the spectators to move away. The transistor was switched off. Conversation, like the low hum of bees, resumed.

'I think it's nauseating,' Selina McKay said.

He hadn't noticed her standing at his side. There were beads of sweat on her temples and she was very pale. He wondered if she had been there long enough to see the whole tableau. Effigy. Television. Placard.

'I suppose we're to blame,' she went on, 'to some extent. I mean we're here.'

He sensed her embarrassment which verged on shame.

Her mouth was twisted in self-contempt. 'I didn't intend coming, but it's on my route home and I . . .'

He cut across her. 'It's natural curiosity.'

'I suppose so. It consoles me a little that you're here, too.'

He didn't know why it should, though he was aware that she spoke honestly. His curiosity was valid. Hers was not. Had her curiosity not been tinged with guilt he would have liked her less. There was, on both sides, a degree of attraction.

She told him that when she arrived ten minutes ago she had seen one of the witnesses in the crowd. 'The dark-haired one who keeps the craft shop. She stayed for five minutes or so, behind the police car. There's a gap in the hedge there and she'd pushed her way forward and got right up to the garden wall. If she felt anything, she didn't show it. I was afraid she'd recognise me as one of the jurors, so I came over here. It wouldn't do for us to meet.'

'No,' Quinn agreed, 'it wouldn't. We jurors

have to be careful what company we keep.'

She sensed mockery and didn't understand it.

He asked her what she thought of the trial so far.

She found the answer difficult to put into words. Carne's marriage had exploded into violence. Her own was dying slowly. It was impossible not to feel some sympathy for him. 'Whatever happened,' she said, 'he's suffering now. You only have to look at him in the dock.'

He wondered what she could see that he couldn't. Carne, apart from brief periods of obvious stress, had himself well in hand.

She rightly interpreted his silence. 'You don't think so?'

'Most of the time he's well in control.'

'That's his training,' she said. She looked over at the house agan. 'When you work for the media—especially with his sort of exposure—it must be a shock when the pack turns vicious.'

He asked her if her work brought her into contact with the public. 'Or don't you work?'

She said she designed jewellery on a freelance basis for a couple of small fashion houses. There was a hint of an apology in her voice. 'If you can call that work. I don't wear my designs. They're for the extroverted and the rich. I don't fit either category.'

It occurred to him that in his youth he had fitted both. His extroverted exploits in the days following Oxford had led to the family money being willed away from him. He hadn't cared then, and he didn't care too much now. Gretl had her own money and Timothy was all right. He was in a good German school and would go on to a good German university if he had that sort of mentality. If he hadn't, he could busk, or set up his own squat.

She cut across her thoughts by asking what he did.

'At one time,' he said, 'I would have reported on what we've just been looking at. I would have added the salt of personal comment—and that would have been acceptable, or not, depending on the editor.'

She noticed he had used the past tense. 'You were once a journalist?'

'Yes.'

'And now?'

'One of the three million catapulted into freedom—and don't commiserate. If I wanted to get up off my ass, I would.'

Selina said nothing.

He asked her if she would like to have a drink with him, or did she have to go home and cook her husband's dinner?

Her husband had gone to a medical conference in Brussels for a week, she told him, and much as she'd like to have a drink with him she had to be home to receive a phone call from her younger son. 'He's just started boarding school and tends to get homesick.' It wasn't an excuse. She wished she could have accepted his invitation. 'It's taking him a while to settle,' she said, 'and I should be home when the call comes through. You understand?'

Yes, he understood. She was a nice woman. A good mother. Not the kind to get her head battered in. He offered her a lift, but she had her own car.

On the drive home Quinn stopped off at a licensed restaurant and had a mixed grill and a couple of beers. He lingered over the meal, and tried to decide just how much he should tell Frances about the scene at her home. Preferably nothing. On the other hand, too bland a picture would be dangerously deceptive. An account of the heavy policing might be sufficient to deter her. Obviously, earlier policing had been lax.

He bought newspapers again and scanned them for any reference to the effigy of Carne. It wasn't mentioned, but it certainly would be tomorrow.

Back in his car, he drove past Hyde Park Corner and noticed that Nils, Stu and Lucille were beating out some musical rubbish to a small appreciative audience. Stu seemed to be playing *pizzicato* on his Strad which was surely bastardising a good instrument. He wondered why Blossom wasn't with them.

Half an hour later, she greeted him in the hallway and pushed him into the living-room with obvious agitation. 'If you look at your statue of Balzac,' she said, almost weeping, 'you will *hit* her.'

'*Hit* her' had come out like a howl from an offended Siamese cat. He looked at her in astonishment. Sartorially superb as ever in bright green silk, her hair immaculately braided, she nevertheless managed to look dishevelled. Due, he realised, to the shattering of her oriental calm. Emotion displayed by Blossom was untidy, and it jarred.

He asked her what she was talking about. She told him that he would see for himself, but that he must be *prepared*. Her gently tinkling voice kept on emphasising words like a piano with loose keys. Frankie had been *drinking* again. She wouldn't *eat*. She wouldn't *talk*. She had spent most of the afternoon sitting by the greenhouse, looking at the *orchids*. Blossom fluttered her delicate little hands and rolled her olive-dark eyes. I was afraid to *leave* her. How could I go and *sing* with the others—and *leave* her?

Blossom's singing was clear and sweet but of no great account. Her absence from the quartet made little difference musically. Her looks were her greatest asset. And now, with emotion flushing her pale golden skin, she was enchanting.

Quinn waited for her to tell him what Frances had done. She didn't attempt to explain, it was too horrific. To Blossom all art was sacrosanct.

110

Even mediocre art. And this wasn't mediocre art. This was a Rodin. A copy—yes. But a copy of a *Rodin*. 'You will forgive her,' she begged, 'she knows not what she does.'

It sounded very Christian. It also sounded very Blossom in a rare moment of stress.

Quinn went to see for himself.

Evening was casting grey shadows over the garden. Which, from Blossom's point of view as she stood anxiously watching him, was just as well. He had collected his statues in the days when he had money to collect them. More cumbersome than paintings, and a nuisance to lug around as his houses became smaller and cheaper, he nevertheless had resisted selling them. His favourites were the Oreades, five nymphs of the mountains and grottoes, sculpted in marble. They were good. Very good. And so was Arion with his lyre. The Rodin hadn't fitted in with the classical theme and he used it to prop up the back fence. It was magnificently solid. If Frances had to paint one of his statues with creosote then she had chosen the right one. It was bad reproduction. He told Blossom it didn't matter and told her to go in. She asked him in a whisper if he was *calm?* He said he was. Very.

He didn't approach Frances but went to sit on the rickety garden bench and watched her in silence. The creosote had a strong smell. He kept it in the shed together with bags of peat and various other garden items. She must have found the paint brush there, too.

Did she have it in her mind as she sloshed creosote over Balzac that she was painting out her father? There was no physical resemblance. Carne had a long narrow face with high cheek bones. Balzac was fleshy and had a moustache. He looked at strong as a bull. Dominating. Carne, even when he was on the box, had never dominated.

The effigy of Carne hadn't looked like him either—a lump of scorched sacking—but there the intention had been plain—a vicious pun on a placard. Carnage. A statement of irrational hate by someone with a twisted mind.

And this?

She was wiping her hands on her jeans. All her movements were careful and slow. She was too drunk to be aware of what she was doing. Impelled by pain. The paternal bond could be a hell of a thing. When you severed it you bled. Frances, emotionally, was haemorrhaging.

After a while she came and sat beside him. A few pale stars were out and the garden was hushed and cool. The orchids, dimly seen through glass, were predatory shapes, colourless.

He told her that he had driven around her house and that she'd be wise to stay away from it for a while. She gave no indication that she had heard him, but slipped her hand in his. It was sticky with creosote and cold.

Later he took her inside and persuaded her to eat some soup and a couple of slices of toast. They were alone in the kitchen. She needed solitude. That she also needed him so that her solitude wasn't complete was becoming obvious.

Nobody had ever needed him this way before. Not even Timothy. He wasn't sure what his role was—just someone of reasonable sensitivity who stayed around, perhaps?

He didn't know how she could eat toast with creosoted hands, but was thankful that she could.

He told her so and for the first time since Nils had brought her home to him, she smiled.

CHAPTER EIGHT

Hester Allendale had dressed for her court appearance with considerable care. Nothing she wore was new. The cream silk dress was one she had worn several times on informal dinner-dates with Carne. He had bought her the matching scarf in Paris when they had weekended there. Latterly she had been highlighting her brown hair with auburn tints. Today the highlights were fair, the way he would remember them. She even wore the same perfume—another of his presents. She needed all the props.

She felt marvellous, exhilarated even. No

stage would be as good as this one. No performance more calculated. She arrived at the Old Bailey in a taxi—less bother than driving her own car and trying to park it—less far to walk through autograph-hunting crowds. The taxi put her down near the entrance. A couple of police officers, anticipating the forward surge of her fans, stood by her protectively and guided her through them. She managed to smile at everyone. Her smile was shy, tentative and utterly charming.

Even Breddon wasn't impervious to it.

'You are Hester Mary Allendale of Flat Number 3, Kingsmond Masions, Bayswater?'

'Yes, that's my London address. I've taken it on a short lease. My permanent home is a cottage in Ashingdon, Essex.' Her diction, like her appearance, was perfect. The public in the gallery leaned forward to catch a better look.

Carne thought she looked pretty good, too. He didn't remember the dress. When you saw Hester naked as often as he had you didn't notice what she wore. He had been anticipating this moment for several days. He had stopped fearing it. Occasionally he wondered if he were being drugged, but his common sense told him he wasn't. Events were tranquillising him; or perhaps stunning was the better word. He had stopped feeling.

Breddon had prepared his material thoroughly. She was a major witness for the prosecution and there was little he didn't know about her. McNair might find a few grey areas, a few stones not yet turned, but he doubted they'd help his client very much. He took her briefly through a résumé of her career, establishing what everyone already knew. She was an actress with that extra indefinable something that made her a popular success. She had no private life. It would have been a high price to pay for some, but not, he guessed, for her.

He took her back two years in time.

'You had just completed a successful season in Stratford in *King Lear*—is that correct?'

'Yes. I played Cordelia—a wonderful part.'

He had read the reviews. She hadn't played it wonderfully, according to some of the more discerning critics, but looking as she did it hadn't really mattered.

'Tell the jury what you did then.'

She turned to them, smiling like a considerate hostess trying to make her guests feel at ease. 'I had planned a holiday. I have friends in Toronto and had hoped to visit them. But the producer of *Arcadia* contacted me and asked if I would do a "one-off" for one of the programmes. I wasn't enthusiastic, until I heard the location. The Western Isles. The filming was to be done in Stromness. It was about the Standing Stones of Stennis and the Neolithic settlement of Skara Brae. Had I been asked to take part in the more

115

usual type of *Arcadia* programme I would have refused, but this one tempted me. I knew the area as I had holidayed there as a child. It's beautiful.'

The judge leaned forward. 'I wonder, Miss Allendale, if you could make your answers rather more brief?' His request was courteous.

'I'm so sorry, my Lord.'

'What part did you play?' Breddon asked.

'No part, really. Just myself. A visitor on holiday being shown the sights.'

'Being shown the sights by the presenter of *Arcadia*—Edward Carne?'

'Correct.'

'Had you met him before?'

'No, it was our first meeting.'

'What happened then?'

'I fell in love with him.' It was shyly spoken. She looked down at her hands.

Carne clapped his hands very softly, almost imperceptibly, and bit back a grin. The word 'love' was for occasions when the public listened. When there had been just the two of them she had referred to sex more robustly.

His first taste of her had been in a caravan with the curtains drawn. Two of the camera crew had been in the adjoining caravan getting drunk on someone's home-brewed beer. Hester had wedged something against the door in case they broke in at the vital moment. The caravan had no key. 'Let copulation thrive,' she had said

116

afterwards, quoting Lear.

Carne interrupted his reverie and began listening to Breddon again, who had moved onwards. The relationship was now established. Had been going on for three months, in fact.

'How frequently did you see Carne when you returned to London?'

'Several times a week.' She was blushing very prettily.

'Was it a sexual relationship?'

'I was in love with him.'

'You're not answering my question.'

'When you love,' she said reproachfully, 'it's natural that the relationship should develop. We slept together—yes.'

'Did he tell you about his wife?'

She sighed. 'I knew he was married, of course. My conscience was troubled, but my feeling for him went very deep. And his for me, or so I thought then.'

And it went on. Carne, the seducer of the innocent, listened without anger. He had forgotten how amusing she could be. And how tantalising. It was difficult now to understand why she had managed to make him so angry in the past. When, he wondered, would she come to the big scene when she had hit him across the jaw with an aerosol bottle of deodorant and he had pushed her head under the bath water?

Without appearing to, Breddon led her up to it in about ten minutes. 'Did you, at any time, go on holiday with Carne?'

'Yes, that same summer, nearly two years ago. We took a very pretty cottage in Brittany for a week. His wife was in the cottage in Wales at the time. He led me to believe she was there with someone else—that she had a lover.'

'*Led* you to believe? Did you subsequently discover it wasn't true?'

'I guess it might not be. I don't know. Jocelyn Carne was showing her age, rather. She didn't seem—well—I don't mean she wasn't attractive—but, a lover? Possible, of course. She was a very pleasant woman.'

'So you had met by then?'

'Once or twice. I don't think she was aware of the "friendship" between her husband and me.'

'The fact that you were lovers?'

She answered coldly. 'Precisely.'

'How would you describe the holiday in France?'

She shrugged. 'It wasn't idyllic. Edward Carne is a man of moods, some of them not pleasant.'

'Can you be more explicit?'

'He was unpredictable. He had a very hot temper.'

'Can you give me an instance of this?'

She looked at the jury for a moment or two in apparent distress and then made an effort to be calm. 'We were meeting friends one evening for dinner at one of the hotels. Edward, at the last minute, didn't want to go. He had been drinking. He wanted to—well, take me to bed. I refused. He went wild.'

'What did he do?' Breddon asked.

'We were in the bathroom. He tried to drown me.'

There was a murmur in the public gallery. The clerk called for order.

'How did you stop him?'

Hester's eyes widened and filled with tears. 'I was completely helpless. I couldn't have stopped him. He was quick to reach flashpoint—and then he'd be calm and rational again. He saw sense—just in time.'

'Did he show you violence on any other occasion?'

'Yes—several times.'

She described the occasions graphically. Some of it was true. All of it was exaggerated and Carne was beginning to get bored. What had Frances called her once? *That pin-headed whore*. He had been annoyed with Frances for stating the obvious.

Breddon asked Hester why she had stayed with Carne when he behaved so badly to her. She explained that he didn't behave badly all the time and that she loved him.

'Even though there must have been times when you were very frightened of him?'

'Yes—one tends to forget the bad times—until they happen again. It's hard to explain. I

119

think he treated his wife the same way. A mutual friend who knew Jocelyn very well told me that she'd noticed bruises...'

Breddon stopped her. 'Only what *you* saw is relevant. Did *you* notice bruises on Mrs Carne?'

'No. I didn't see her frequently enough.'

'Did you intend marrying Carne if he divorced his wife?'

'Yes. We spoke of it. I know now that he didn't mean it.'

Breddon looked at her thoughtfully. 'When you realised the relationship wasn't going to be put on a permanent basis, did you feel animosity towards Carne—or to his wife?'

'Animosity?' She tasted the word as if it surprised her. 'Why, no. I thought in the early days of the relationship that I would have liked to marry him and have children. I know now that it would have been fatal. I've had a lucky escape. I'm grateful.'

'When you use the word "fatal", do you mean it literally? A fatal accident, for instance, implies a deadly accident. Is that what you intended to imply?'

'In view of what he did to his wife,' Hester said, 'then the answer to your question is yes.'

McNair got up quickly. 'I must object. Nothing has yet been proved against my client.'

The judge agreed. 'Stay with the facts as you know them, Miss Allendale.'

Breddon glanced at his notes. 'Can you tell

120

the court where you were on the twenty-fifth of June last year?'

She frowned. 'The twenty-fifth of June? I'm afraid dates don't mean very much to me. Where was I supposed to be on the twenty-fifth of June?'

'Were you staying in Carne's cottage in Snowdonia?' Breddon asked blandly. If she denied it, he could produce a witness.

She didn't deny it. 'Of course. I'd forgotten. We had a weekend together there.'

'Just the two of you?'

'Yes.'

'Was Jocelyn Carne aware of this?'

'I don't know. I think she had gone somewhere with her daughter.'

'Weren't you taking a chance, you and Carne, using the family's holiday cottage as a love-nest?' He used the word with heavy irony.

She looked at him steadily. 'It was foolish, perhaps. When you love someone you sometimes behave thoughtlessly.'

'Had you been there before?'

'No. It was the first time.'

'The weather was kind to you? Were you able to go walking?'

Spencer-Leigh, about to comment on the irrelevancy of the question, realised that it wasn't irrelevant at all. He listened to the answer.

'Yes, of course we went walking. It's

beautiful country.'

'So you got to know the environs of the cottage quite well that weekend?'

'I suppose so—yes.'

'You are aware that Jocelyn Carne's body was hidden within walking distance of the cottage?'

'It was reported in the newspapers. Everyone knows.'

Breddon's tempo began to quicken. 'When you and Carne went walking that weekend did Carne say anything to you about doing away with his wife?'

'Certainly not. He might have thought it. Had he said it I would have walked out on him immediately.'

'Had he said it to you later—after the act of murder—and told you where the body was buried, would you have informed the police then?'

'Of course I would.' Her distress now wasn't simulated.

Spencer-Leigh intervened. 'Would you re-phrase your last question, Mr Breddon?'

'I'm sorry, my Lord.' Breddon re-phrased it. 'Did Carne tell you he had murdered his wife?'

'No.'

'Did you make an anonymous phone call to the police stating that he had?'

'No.'

'You have told the court of Carne's violence on several occasions. How was his behaviour towards you on that weekend?'

She considered it. 'He was moody—rather depressed.'

'Some six weeks afterwards, in the middle of August, did you attend a clinic in Birmingham and have your pregnancy terminated?'

She was startled and then deeply angry. 'I didn't expect you to...' She halted. 'Yes.'

'Was the child Carne's?'

'Of course.'

'Did he agree to the abortion?'

'He insisted on it. He had his precious television image to preserve. He would do anything to remain untarnished in the eyes of his fans. A normal man would have had a divorce. Or he would have encouraged me to have the baby. Not Carne.' All gentleness had gone from her voice. The words were clipped and sharp with venom.

'So he encouraged you to behave violently towards your unborn child?'

McNair again appealed to Spencer-Leigh. 'My learned friend is using unnecessarily emotive language. The abortion of a foetus is hardly an act of violence against an unborn child.'

Spencer-Leigh thought it was, but kept his strongly-held moral views to himself. 'I understand the point you're making,' he said to Breddon, 'but I think there might have been undue exaggeration. Do you need to continue that line of questioning?'

Breddon didn't. Carne and Hester Allendale had been surprisingly careless. Some strong emotion must have coloured the relationship at some stage.

Carne, looking across the court at Hester, remembered the weekend in question very well. She had forgotten to bring her contraceptive pills and had rummaged around crossly in the bathroom cupboard hoping that Jocelyn had left hers behind. He had reminded her that he and Jocelyn hadn't had sex for a long time and, as far as he knew, she hadn't any pills.

'That pathetic, bloody woman!' she had stormed. They had gone to bed and chanced it. Later, they had both agreed to the abortion. He had paid for it.

He began listening to the evidence again.

'During the long period of Jocelyn's disappearance,' Breddon said to Hester, 'did your relationship with Carne grow closer?'

She was calm again now and in full control of herself. 'No. On the contrary. I began to feel uneasy with him. He seemed to be brooding about something. He'd start to say something, then stop. He looked at me sometimes as if . . . well, I don't know. He frightened me and I began to make excuses not to meet him.'

'I see.' She had said it beautifully. Breddon couldn't hope for more. 'Thank you, Miss Allendale. No further questions.' He sat down.

McNair rose to cross-examine. He smiled pleasantly at Hester. She looked at him warily and then smiled tentatively back.

'It's quite an ordeal, isn't it,' he said disarmingly, 'all this rather unpleasant probing into what should be a very private relationship between a man and a woman?'

She agreed. 'But the relationship is over.'

'Quite. And you have escaped unscathed.'

'Apart from emotional scars.'

'Ah,' he said, 'emotional scars. But just for a little, if you'll bear with me, I should like to know more about your physical scars. Carne was violent, you tell us. Did you attend your doctor as a result of bruising, perhaps?'

'There was some bruising. I coped with it myself.'

He nodded approvingly. 'A brave lady. But if it came to a broken bone—or temporary concussion, say—you then called in medical help?'

She was careful not to show her anger. 'It wasn't that bad.'

'So he didn't beat you about the head—or break any bones. Splendid. Was he a flagellator, perhaps? Did he use a whip?'

'I wouldn't have permitted it. I'm sexually normal. I'm not a masochist.'

'And it takes two to play,' McNair agreed. 'So my client isn't a sadist?'

She didn't answer.

125

'Yes, or no, Miss Allendale. I want to be quite clear about this.'

'He could be very violent.'

'So you kept telling my learned friend. Would you agree that some roughness between lovers doesn't amount to sadism, that you were, in fact, exaggerating?'

'He tried to drown me.'

He pursed his lips as if biting back a smile. 'Yes—the drowning. I was coming to that. In the bathroom, I believe, not the open sea. He could, of course, have drowned you there quite easily. George Joseph Smith disposed of his wives that way in nineteen fifteen ... Were you in the bath at the time?'

'No. I'd just got out. He pushed my head in.'

'You mean he dunked you—like an apple in a tub. Had you been teasing him?'

Her face was flushed. 'We had been quarrelling. I've already explained.'

'You wanted to go to the dinner-party and he wanted to make love to you. So he pushed your pretty head in the water. Just long enough, perhaps, to make a mess of your hair. Awfully violent, wasn't it? Very odd behaviour for a lover! What did he do after that—rape you?'

'I wouldn't per ...'

He cut in sharply. 'Permit? No, of course you wouldn't. You were always fully in control. You must have been a rather exasperating lady at times, Miss Allendale, and you are certainly a lady who exaggerates. There's a lot of difference between love-play and sadism. My client was in love with you. He may have behaved boisterously at times—childishly—perhaps even roughly. But had there been true violence in the accepted sense you would have gone for medical help.'

'You're naturally biased in your client's favour,' Hester said icily.

'And you're quite obviously biased against him,' McNair retorted. 'I think we're coming to the emotional scars now, aren't we? Let's have a look at them.'

She waited suspiciously.

'No one is disputing the fact that you were carrying Carne's child. You both agreed to abort it. As a successful actress you could afford to bring up a child on your own if necessary. You chose not to. *You*—and I emphasise it—chose not to. Whether Carne tried to influence you or not is neither here nor there. You were the mother. The choice was yours. So you aborted it. Very well. No one blames you. Equally no one should blame Carne. Even so, I'm prepared to believe that there might have been an emotional scar. Afterwards, were you very upset?'

'Yes, of course I was.'

'Psychologically a little disturbed perhaps?'

'I don't know what you mean.'

'Can you recall an incident during a first-night party in early December, the opening night of your new play at the Lyric Theatre?'

Her tension was mounting. 'No.'

'Oh, come, I'm sure you must. Carne was your guest and very ungallantly he spent a large part of the evening with your understudy. Most of the cast witnessed the ensuing quarrel. You drove home on your own—recklessly—and had your licence endorsed.'

'I don't know what that has to do with the present case.' She turned to the judge, 'My Lord...'

'It's perfectly valid to try to prove that your client might not be as violent as the witness has made out, Mr McNair,' Spencer-Leigh said, 'but I'm rather unclear as to what you're attempting to show the court now?'

McNair justified the continuing validity of his questions. 'I'm trying to show that the witness's vilification of her former lover could be due to the emotional trauma of an abortion, followed by the cooling-off of Carne's affections for her.'

Spencer-Leigh frowned. 'It's an hypothesis, only. It might be acceptable if voiced by a psychologist, but even then I should have reservations. Miss Allendale is a witness, she is not on trial. Her state of mind is not a matter for the court. If you continue with your questioning I must advise you to stay with the facts.'

Had McNair heeded the judge, his defence might have been of some use. Unwisely, he pressed on.

'Isn't it true, Miss Allendale, that during the months following the abortion of your child, Edward Carne's interest in you began to wane? He was seen escorting other women on several occasions. The counsel for the prosecution asked you if your relationship with Carne grew closer during Jocelyn's absence from the scene. Your reply was, and I quote:' he read from his notes, '"On the contrary. I began to feel uneasy with him. He seemed to be brooding about something. He'd start to say something—then stop. He looked at me sometimes as if . . . well, I don't know . . . He frightened me." And then you added: "I started to make excuses not to meet him." Wouldn't you agree that the truth was he had started making excuses not to meet you? The word "frightened" wasn't a good choice—"aggrieved" would have been more precise. You were aggrieved, as any woman is when she senses the cooling-off and imminent departure of a lover. You were uneasy with him because he was uneasy with you. It's difficult to end a relationship. He'd try to put his feelings into words—and then stop. For fear of hurting you, probably. He was gradually pushing you out of his life. Quite naturally you felt both pain and malice. You wanted to get back at him— and so you did. Even though you are under oath you have done your best to blacken Carne. The reaction of a woman scorned, perhaps? He tired of you, Miss Allendale. Your affair was over.'

She was almost sick with humiliation and trembling with rage. Even so, when she spoke her voice was controlled and carried complete conviction. 'Edward Carne murdered his wife,' she said. 'I know it here,' she touched her forehead, 'and I know it here,' she touched the cream silk dress just under her left breast.

It was pure theatre, effective and damning.

McNair, aware that he had played Breddon's hand for him, deplored his lack of foresight. 'Heart and mind?' he asked sarcastically. 'Or malice and imagination. Pretty gestures and dramatic statements are part of your stock-in-trade as an actress. As a witness they carry no weight at all.'

He knew that Breddon would ask the necessary questions arising from this, so was forced to ask them himself.

'Were you lying when my learned friend asked you if Carne had told you he had murdered his wife—and your answer was "No"? Think hard before answering me now.'

'He didn't tell me.' Her denial sounded like a lie. Deliberately, he wondered?

'So you're not guilty of perjury?'

'No.'

'I believe you,' McNair said. 'I have absolutely no reason not to. Had I ever doubted Edward Carne's innocence I would have awaited your answer with considerable trepidation.'

He sat down, after a quick glance at Breddon who was looking unbearably smug.

Breddon didn't wish to re-examine Miss Allendale. The status quo was near perfect. Perfection would have been Hester's admitting perjury which, of course, the wily dame wouldn't. He wondered what the time lapse was between Carne's confession and her haring off to the nearest telephone to alert the police.

And Quinn, together with most of the jury, was wondering the same thing.

* * *

When Hester left the witness-box the spectators in the public gallery felt cheated. From their point of view it wasn't good stage-craft to produce the star of the performance in the first act and then banish her to the wings. The supporting cast, Carne's liaisons over the past three years, tended to bore. There were two of them: Kim Sydenham, a production assistant at Broadcasting House, and Jane Sinclair, a freelance photographer married to a junior Cabinet Minister. Carne had bedded them, tired of them and left them. In each case the gossip columnists had squeezed the situation dry. Both women were bitter and gave their evidence in short, caustic sentences. Carne's catholicity of taste rather than any latent tendency he might have towards murder was made evident by their testimony. In looks and temperament they were totally different. Kim, a quiet introverted woman of thirty, gave the impression of unassailable virtue. Jane, a couple of years older, plump and pretty, did not.

Carne listened to them—on and off. Intimacy was difficult to recollect. Time clothed nudity and cooled passion. If the dead returned, physically intact, after a long period of absence, they would be greeted with polite reserve.

Even Jocelyn.

He turned her name over in his mind. There was no person behind it. He tried to make an anagram out of the name and failed. His brain was woolly. He felt perilously near sleep.

When the last witness of the day entered the witness-box Carne became slowly aware of his surroundings again. How had Breddon caught this one in the prosecution net, he wondered? Unease eroded his calm. He leaned forward, elbows on his knees, his chin resting on his clenched fists, and began listening.

She could have nothing to do with Carne's sexual life—a fact that the jury realised before she began to speak. She was a self-assured, middle-aged spinster with cropped grey hair, an aquiline nose and a gentle, mobile mouth. Her diction, like Hester Allendale's, was clear but her stage, unlike Hester's, was the school-room. She gave her name as Helen Naylor. She explained that she had a degree in education and that she was the head of a small, private establishment for girls who had, for one reason or another, opted out of the state educational system and were aiming for university.

'A crammer?' Bredden asked.

It was a description she didn't like. 'I educate—I do not force-feed with indigestible facts.'

Breddon apologised and invited her to tell the court how she came to meet the defendant.

'Mr and Mrs Carne brought their daughter, Frances, to my school after there had been some trouble at her previous one. She was a child who could be disruptive. The Carnes didn't believe that the state system was right for her. They had been particularly resentful because an educational psychologist had interviewed her on a couple of occasions without their permission.' She glanced at Carne who looked away from her. She spoke to Breddon again. 'The policy of my school is to work with the parents—to get to know the home background. To understand a problem is to solve it.'

'And the problem in this particular case...?' Breddon asked.

'Adolescent instability, exacerbated by the father's rise to fame. There was a change in life-style. The small close-knit unit of the Bristol home was eroded. The family moved here to London. A change of house. A change of school. The encroachment of curious and insensitive fans. So many factors.'

'I see.' Breddon looked at his notes. 'Would you tell the court what occurred one evening three years ago, during the summer term?'

Helen Naylor once again looked at Carne and her eyes held his. This time she addressed him directly. 'I'm sorry,' she said, 'but it has to be told. Standing here in this witness-box doesn't give me any joy, believe me.'

Spencer-Leigh intervened. 'You must not address the defendant, Miss Naylor.'

She sparked with sudden anger. 'I'm just trying to make it plain that I am forced by a subpoena to be here, my Lord.' She turned back to Breddon. 'I have thirty pupils and two members of staff. Of the thirty pupils—all girls—a small number board. Frances Carne attended daily. The incident you want to know about occurred about seven-thirty on a Saturday evening. Frances arrived with a packed suitcase. She was crying. Home, she said, was intolerable. She had come to stay. I failed to get a lucid statement from her. She was too upset. Naturally I phoned her parents. When they arrived an hour or so later, I persuaded Frances to go to my study and speak to them alone. It was a mistake on my part. I should have been there. The parents seemed quite calm and controlled. They were not and I should have sensed it. I didn't.'

Carne remembered the scene in the study all

too clearly. The three of them had sat around a small mahogany table, trying to talk. Or rather, Jocelyn had been talking—forcing them to listen. Her words of sweet bloody reason had dripped like paraffin on smouldering wood.

Helen Naylor paused, reluctant to go on.

'Yes?' Breddon asked. 'And so what happened?'

'I don't know what happened.' Her reply was brusque. 'I was in one of the class-rooms across the hall. Frances screamed. And then Mrs Carne came out of the study—she stumbled—looked vaguely around her for the front door and then went down the steps into the road. She walked into the path of a car. She wasn't badly hurt. The case came to court and the driver was exonerated. Medical evidence showed a blow to the face that had dazed her. She refused to say how she had come by it. There was a newspaper report—unfortunately. If the fracas had been ignored, I wouldn't be standing here now.' She sighed and shook her head ruefully. 'The price of fame is lack of privacy. We, the rest of us, may squabble as bitterly as we please without being accorded an inch of newsprint.' She turned to the jury. 'It may interest you to know that Frances returned home and seemed to ride out that particular storm without being too emotionally hurt by it.'

'Until her mother was murdered,' Breddon said harshly, 'and she left home finally, but not, this time, to take refuge with you.'

'No,' Helen Naylor agreed, 'not with me.' She hadn't seen Frances since she had left for university—a fact that she had told both the police and the press—and, much earlier, Frances's father.

'Rather damning, wouldn't you say,' Breddon suggested, 'that she hasn't come forward to give evidence on her father's behalf?' And then, before she could reply or Spencer-Leigh interject, he abruptly dismissed the witness. 'That's all, Miss Naylor, thank you.'

McNair, sensing sympathy in this reluctant witness, ventured to cross-examine.

'In your evidence you have shown that Mr Carne accompanied his wife on visits to the school. The mother could have visited alone, but did not. Would this suggest to you that not only was he a caring father, but he was also a supportive husband, at least in relation to their child?'

She seemed thankful to be able to say something in Carne's favour. 'Why, certainly. They both cared deeply for Frances.'

'Would it seem natural to you, knowing her as you did, that her absence from the court is due to a deep love for her father, that it would pain her too much to see him in such harrowing circumstances?'

Breddon, annoyed at the drift of McNair's cross-examination, was about to object but then decided to remain silent.

She answered reluctantly and honestly. 'I think her affection was mainly for her mother. She looked like her mother. Spoke like her. There wasn't the usual animosity that you find between a teen-age girl and her mother. I don't say she wasn't fond of her father. It was obvious to me that she was. But her mother was the favourite parent. That was plain to see.'

McNair tried to lay the stress where it should be laid. 'Children, and I speak from personal knowledge, tend to favour first one parent and then the other. They're ambivalent with their affection. You say she was obviously fond of her father. After the family row in the school, she went home and, in your words, "rode out the storm without being too emotionally hurt". I put it to you that it was a normal household with the usual ups and downs. Had it not been so, she would have persuaded her parents to let her board at your school and not have returned home so willingly.'

He decided to stop with that statement. How many members of the jury had normal households, he wondered? Amongst that randomly picked bunch of individuals in the jury box, was there anyone prepared to believe in the myth of Carne's normal household? It was a pity that today's evidence had pushed Frances into the limelight. Her desertion would be a new angle for the press. More vigorous efforts would

be made to find her. For Carne's sake he hoped
they wouldn't succeed.

CHAPTER NINE

Quinn heard the morning paper being pushed
through the letter-box and went down to
retrieve it before anyone else had the chance. On
the doormat beside it was a birthday card from
Timothy. Quinn had forgotten it was his
birthday but was pleased that Timothy hadn't.
The card showed a man fishing in a stream and
hooking up a barrel of beer. It was apt. Last
night he'd had a bit of a booze-up. Nothing
dramatic. He'd been in no particular hurry to go
home. He'd felt he couldn't cope with Frances.
His mind refused to form comforting phrases.
The day's evidence had made her public
property, she was no longer his alone. The other
jury members, strongly aware of her, were
talking about her speculatively. 'When it's one
of your own blood,' he had heard Selina say to
Elaine Balfour, 'you expect loyalty.' 'But loyalty
to whom?' Elaine had asked. 'If I had murdered
my son's father, would my son stand by me?'
Both women had turned to him for comment,
but he had refused to be drawn.

'To Dad,' Timothy had written on the card,
'with love.' Well, that was something. It was

more than something. He wondered if Gretl had prodded him into writing it, or if he'd written it off his own bat. Anyway, it was there. A smudged scrawl. Good to see. There was more writing on the back. 'There's a parcel in the post. Hope it comes on the day.' It hadn't, unless it came later, whatever it was.

Quinn's mild hangover receded. He almost felt happy. He took the card up to his bedroom and then sat on the side of the bed and skimmed through the morning paper. The account of the trial was still making the front page. Hester Allendale's evidence took up two columns. A third column reported the evidence of the other witnesses of the day, finishing with a couple of sentences about Frances. 'The accused's daughter has not appeared in court. Her presence in the witness-box could considerably influence the outcome of the trial—one way or the other.' It was pithy. A neat summing-up. On the inside page were two photographs, a studio portrait of Hester and a clear and quite pleasant snap of Jocelyn. Quinn looked at it thoughtfully. She had wanted a photograph of her mother. This one shouldn't upset her.

As he dressed he wondered if there had been any trauma during the previous evening. He hadn't wanted to know and had gone straight up to his room. Today he felt ready to face her again.

He tapped on her door. 'I'm going to court,

shortly. You might like to see the morning paper before I leave. There's a picture of your mother in it.'

She didn't answer and he pushed the door open gently. She was pretending to be asleep. The duvet had fallen on the floor. It was patterned with koala bears. He wished his son was lying tousle-headed on the under-sheet with eyes determinedly closed against the new day. Timothy had always got up with alacrity when there was no school. Tomorrow there would be no court and for the whole of the weekend he would have the responsibility of Frances.

He didn't want it.

For the first time in his life he wanted a neat home in suburbia, with a small lawn to cut and an undemanding mistress who would cosset him. He didn't want a decaying house full of buskers and a small, thin girl who hid the empties under the bed.

Just one empty, he noticed. Gin. He picked it up and put it on the dressing-table. And then he picked up the duvet and put it over her flat stomach and carefully arranged legs.

'It's here,' he said, as he used to say to Timothy, 'the new day. You can't stop the sun. It might even warm you. Try it.'

She opened her eyes slowly. They were dark brown and the whites were bloodshot. Gin? Tears? Both?

He told her she needed fresh air. 'You should

take a brisk walk.'

'I can't go out.'

'Damn it,' he said, exasperated, 'there aren't police posted at every corner ready to pounce on you and haul you into the witness-box.'

'There might be. I can't risk it. Stop talking about it. I don't want to talk about it.'

He didn't want to talk about it either, but it would have to be discussed soon. Some time this weekend. The trial wouldn't last much longer. The jury would be considering the verdict in a few days. At least Daddy wouldn't die—just rot slowly at Her Majesty's pleasure.

He wondered how she would react to a verdict of guilty. Dance with delight?

Or not.

She had noticed the newspaper at the foot of the bed and was eyeing it as if it were a spider. 'How does she look?'

'Your mother? Like you when you've combed your hair and brushed your teeth and put your clothes on. It's a head and shoulders snapshot taken in a garden somewhere; there's a tree behind her.'

She half-moved towards the paper and then stopped.

'Is he in it, too?'

'No—but on the same page there's one of Hester Allendale.'

'That bitch!'

'Yes, that bitch.'

141

She picked up the paper and began reading. He wondered if he should go downstairs and leave her to it. She might need him, so better stay. He went over to the window and looked down at his statues. Apart from Balzac, there was a pleasant golden sheen of morning on them. Balzac, from this angle, glowered blackly, a head on a severed torso. Later, he'd push it behind the shed. The orchids, bright as tropical birds, shone in the sunlight. It was going to be a hot day. The greenhouse windows must be opened. Blossom, dressed in amber silk, was shooing off next-door's moggy. It was eating something on Arion's lyre. Now it was jumping from statue to statue, it had dropped whatever it was. A piece of bacon? A mouse? Not a mouse. Blossom wouldn't be so calm. She was picking it up fastidiously with a leaf. Now she was putting it in the bin. Stu was coming out and saying something to her. They were going in together. Breakfast ready, probably. Today it was Nils's turn to cook. He did it rather well. The buskers did most things rather well, including living in a parentless vacuum. If they were perceptive of Frances's pain, and he believed they were, they had achieved a nice balance between sympathy and indifference—with the exception of Blossom. Blossom shared herself out like a cake. A slice of sex for him. A slice of sisterly concern for Frances. That the main part of the cake went to Stu must have been of some consolation to him. His attitude towards her largesse to others was heroic.

He turned to see how Frances was reacting to the account of yesterday's court proceedings. Had McNair been his counsel he'd have sacked him. Breddon had looked like a chess-player whose opponent had destroyed his own queen. As for Carne, he had the appearance of a spectator who had bets on both sides. He had even smiled at Hester as she left the witness-box. The smile had shocked her. She had recoiled as if he had swiped her across the jaw.

Was he, perhaps, a little mad? If so—why not a plea of guilty, but with diminished responsibility?

Frances was still reading. Reading and re-reading, he guessed. She was no paler than usual. She wasn't looking for the gin bottle. Timothy's bed was small, but she fitted it. She was exactly ten years older than Timothy—and nineteen years younger than him.

His stomach crawled with compassion for her.

After a few minutes, she spoke. 'It's bad for him, isn't it?'

'Not good.'

He waited to see if she had any comment on this—any query about how her father was looking. She was silent but Quinn knew that her abandonment of him wasn't cold-blooded. There was grief and there was rage.

Understandable. Of course she didn't want to go into the witness-box.

Nor did he want to depart for court. That his anomalous position in the jury might eventually land him in the dock didn't worry him too much. That was for the future. His conscience didn't baulk at the illegality of the situation, but it baulked at emotional manipulation. Not that she was consciously manipulating him. She hadn't deliberately left the torn-up newspaper photograph of her father where he could find it. She wasn't deliberately fingering her mother's photograph now like a blind person reading a love poem in braille.

He told her abruptly to get up and go down for breakfast. 'Afterwards—if you won't go out, at least sit in the garden. Do a bit of useful weeding or something, but for Christ's sake, don't creosote anything else.'

He touched her shoulder, small and bony, under her borrowed nightdress. 'Try not to worry.'

★   ★   ★

On this, the fifth day of the trial, McNair presented witnesses for the defence. They were not impressive. Carne's loyalty, industry and talent were not in dispute. His 'sunny disposition' as one former employer unfortunately put it, was no proof that he was incapable of murder. You could be kind to your colleague in the morning and kill your wife in the afternoon. He needed an alibi for the night of the fire. There wasn't one. As a last resource he needed someone close to him to stand up in the witness-box and say that murder was totally out of character—someone like his daughter. When McNair had told him that she'd gone to ground somewhere and couldn't be found, he hadn't seemed unduly perturbed but now he was puzzled by Carne's seeming lack of anxiety. Surely, he should feel some concern but latterly he didn't seem to be worried about anything. To look anxious and remorseful mightn't do him any good with the jury, but his present bland indifference was even worse.

McNair told Carne that he would only put him in the witness-box if he could come up with something over the weekend that would strengthen his case. 'Think about it. The defence is already too fragile without your crumbling under Breddon's questioning. If you're shielding someone, I've got to know. What about that woman from the craft centre— Olivia Mason? If you were bedding down with her somewhere while poor sick hubby was having a heart attack, then tell me.'

Carne's expression was difficult to interpret. His eyes had narrowed momentarily and then he had seemed amused. 'A beautiful woman,' he said, 'a tempting idea, but the answer is no.'

Shock and amusement didn't normally blend, but in Carne, for a moment or two, they had.

The possibility that he might have taken Hester Allendale to the cottage on the night in question had been dismissed early on during the preliminary investigations. She had been on stage in the city of York until gone eleven and had been roused from her bed just before four in the morning by the hotel firebell—a false alarm, but a useful alibi nevertheless.

McNair told Carne that he and Richardson, his solicitor, would have another discussion with him at Brixton on Saturday evening. 'In the meantime consider your situation. The evidence against you is mostly circumstantial, but it's strong enough to bring in a verdict of guilty.'

Carne agreed to think everything over 'very seriously'. It was polite and placatory.

'Goddammit, man,' McNair exploded with uncharacteristic rage, 'you're the one who's facing a life-sentence, not me. Start helping yourself while there's still time.'

The judge's advice to the jury as the court rose for the weekend was predictable. He hoped they would have a restful couple of days and avoid anything or anybody that might be prejudicial to the case. 'You must keep your minds clear, ladies and gentlemen. Discussion blunts the issue at this stage. Excessive reading of the tabloids has the same effect. Avoid contentious situations. The opinions of others

146

are biased, so don't listen to them. Your own opinions are not yet fully formed—they can't be, until you have listened intently to the closing speeches and then weighed up the evidence. It might be unrealistic to ask you not to discuss the case with your families, nevertheless I do ask it of you. In the past you would have been separated from everyone. Nowadays you are trusted to behave honourably and circumspectly.'

The jury, looking suitably solemn, embraced two days of freedom and planned how to use them.

Professor Leary hoped to get more work done on his book. A chapter on crime and punishment in ancient Knossos might be worth the effort of even more research. The idea appealed to him.

Sam Jacobson had a great longing to play some peaceful music. It had been a disturbing week. He had endured it unhappily. Now, more than ever, he thanked God for his wife and beautiful daughters. They would, perhaps, make another beautiful daughter—or even, if God willed, a son—during this respite from the trial. He had been too anxious all the week and had quite failed as a man. All that talk of violence and sexual matters had unnerved him.

James Cornwallis had promised to examine the possibility of installing a downstairs bathroom in Irene Sinclair's house. He understood that she lived with her elderly arthritic sister who climbed stairs with difficulty. Miss Sinclair, despite her rather authoritative manner, was pleasant enough to talk to. They had discussed Germany and the last war over a cup of coffee in the Old Bailey canteen. She had quoted something in German by a bloke called Nietzsche. About superman. Carne, they both agreed, was no superman. He couldn't remember how she had turned the conversation to bathrooms after that, but somehow she had. He didn't mind. Weekends were lonely and he liked his work.

Colin Middler intended having a working weekend, too. His wife had booked in some extra chiropody patients for Saturday, including a nail-wedge resection. The patient was garrulous and would pump him. Unless, of course, her own minor blood-flow would take her mind off Carne's more spectacular blood-letting. The fact that it was probably illegal to treat patients whilst drawing jury subsistence didn't bother him. He had mislaid the rules. Deliberately.

Peter Lomax, who had a more tender conscience, had a painting to finish—a copy of a Turkish miniature he'd seen in the Topkapi Museum in Istanbul on one of his carpet-buying trips. Next week when the trial was over, as it promised to be, he would return to the store. The taboo on conversation would be lifted by then. He wondered what the verdict would be. His mind, so far, was commendably empty.

The two young members of the jury, Trina Thompson and Sarah Gayland, were going to spend Saturday morning moving Trina's boy-friend's belongings into Sarah's flat. The arrangement suited both of them. Trina's father was due to arrive by the afternoon train. Sarah's errant dentist might arrive any time and it would amuse her to disconcert him. All the talk of Carne's lovers had made her randy. She was careful to conceal this from Trina who thought she was being extremely kind. Her naïvety astonished Sarah. Did she honestly believe that her rather good-looking and obviously long-suffering social worker-trainee was going to sleep on the *floor?*

William Dalton, deprived by his reptiles from company of any sort, contemplated a solitary weekend and decided to sleep through most of it. He had been forced to get up early every day; it would make a change to lie in. He wondered what time Carne got booted out of bed in Brixton. The squalor that the smooth Brit must be suffering gave him pleasure. Jocelyn Carne's murder reminded him of his family's bloody demise on the lonely Rhodesian farm. Carne and the tribesmen had something in common. And he felt a great, though irrational, rage against him because of the association.

Elaine Balfour had no plans for the weekend.

She would have liked to invite Selina McKay over for lunch but decided not to embarrass her with an invitation she might not want to accept. A gift of ear-plugs plus sympathy at the right time shouldn't force social obligations on the recipient. All the same, she would have enjoyed turning out a good meal and sharing it with her. And talking about Carne. No matter what the judge might say, she needed to talk. She had dreamt about Carne last night. He had been sitting in a dark room—a cell? His face, a white smudge like crumpled paper, had been lit momentarily by the headlamps of a passing car. And then the darkness had obliterated him. She was anxious about the outcome of the trial and wanted no further part in it. Had she been stricken by a genuine illness she would have welcomed it. Too honest to plead sick when she wasn't, she knew she would have to soldier on.

Unknown to her, Selina had toyed with the idea of asking her over to her home, but had desisted on the offchance that Quinn might be invited instead. If this were a menopausal heightening of the libido then she could put the blame on nature. If the word 'blame' applied. She didn't understand herself. His proximity in the jury box both comforted and disturbed her. With each passing day of the trial she was becoming more aware of him. In her saner moments she felt a strong surge of guilt that her mind wasn't focused where it should be—

solely on Carne. It was a small consolation that the burden of decision didn't rest wholly on her.

By the time the court had cleared, the afternoon sunlight had mellowed to a deep orange so that the goddess of justice at the top of the Bailey seemed aflame. The jurors, aloof and self-conscious, were like a separate species, each making his exit through the crowd of sightseers and reporters.

Carne, barely conscious of them, sat in the prison van and felt the sun warm the back of his neck. McNair's glum predictions of disaster were like the low mutterings of a hostile sea. Enclosed in its depths, like a pearl stuck fast in the flesh of an oyster, was Frances. Frances *now*. His grown-up daughter; living through the most appalling period of her life. He couldn't take on the burden of her pain. He hadn't that sort of strength. Wherever she was, whatever she was doing, it was essential that he should feel no pity, no anxiety, no anger. So live in the faraway past where all was normal. Make images like set-pieces on a stage and walk into them. Once upon a time. A holiday on a farm. Smell of clover and cow dung. Eight-year-old Frances playing with the farm cat. Playing gently. Jocelyn, beside her, watchful. Jocelyn wearing sandals of straw; the blue veins of her feet prominent under the skin. Image too strong. Fade her. Blur her. Get rid of her. Now just Frances and himself in the days of tranquillity.

Frances long gone. Young. Safe. Held tenderly by time. Keep it so. Keep away. *Don't come near me.*

The van was revving up and above the noise of the traffic he heard the music of 'Greensleeves', the *Arcadia* signature tune, and believed he was imagining it. The van gathered speed and the music was lost. The prison officer was looking at him curiously. Had he been speaking out loud? Or looking as crazy as he felt? He smiled at him pleasantly.

Quinn, too, was smiling. The buskers were audacious to ply their trade here. They were a bright blob of colour as they made their way along Newgate Street. Lucille was wearing a Spanish outfit, crimson skirt and a dark green bolero. Her voice was strong and throaty, brazen as a bell. Blossom, still in amber silk, couldn't be heard at all, but she didn't need to be. Her lovely little body was like molten gold as she moved to the music. Stu's Stradivarius made more of the tune than it deserved. Nils's guitar was a thrumming undertone. The crowd looked at the departing van and then turned all their attention to the buskers. Some began to hum. There were ribald remarks. Laughter. Blossom began darting in and out of the crowd holding out her black felt money-bag embroidered with flowers. It was a capacious bag and could hold a considerable amount of loot but without the givers being aware of just how well the buskers

152

were doing. They wouldn't do well here, Quinn guessed. He gave them three minutes before the police moved them on.

Selina had noticed Quinn standing on the edge of the pavement. She went over and joined him. 'It's a haunting tune.'

He didn't answer immediately. Olivia Mason was on the opposite side of the road. Today her hair was loose, falling around a ribbon of bitter green. Her homespun dress was the colour of weathered pebbledash. Her clothes didn't enhance her, but then she didn't need enhancement. Her beauty was a stark statement of fact. She was watching the buskers sombrely.

And then the police came and the buskers were off, departing swiftly, Stu's Stradivarius held high out of harm's way, Nils equally careful of his guitar, the girls careful of nothing other than catching the coins.

'Yes,' Quinn said to Selina.

She had forgotten what she had said to him.

'Rather bad taste,' she commented, 'playing Carne's tune right here.'

'Deplorable,' he agreed. 'Do you suppose Henry played it when his queens were decapitated?'

She sensed anger and was disconcerted.

'Attractive youngsters,' she observed, 'but you'd think they'd have something better to do.'

Such as staying home and looking after Frances, he thought. And Quinn realised that it was time he got back to her.

He told Selina that he hoped she would have a pleasant weekend. Puzzled by his brusqueness she wished him the same.

He had gone a couple of paces when he turned back.

'In their spare time,' he said, 'they tend the wounded.'

'Who do?' She was startled.

But he turned and went again without answering.

CHAPTER TEN

On Saturday Frances spent half an hour helping Quinn water his orchids—and several hours sitting on a tattered deckchair in the greenhouse. A mean wind scurried around the statuary. Inside, the greenhouse was humid with a strong smell of wet earth. A rowan tree near the house shaded the orchids from too much direct sun. Quinn observing her from the living-room window, thought she looked like a disconsolate mole in the middle of a tropical forest. The colours, bright and gorgeous, blazed around her. *Shouted* at her. How could she bear to sit in there feeling as she did, he wondered? She had a book on her lap but wasn't reading it. It was impossible, he had discovered, to sit amongst orchids and read. It was a place for switching off your mind and letting vibrant nature tingle your skin like a jacuzzi.

The buskers were away attending a pop festival. They would return mid-week, glassy-eyed from drugs and dirty after sleeping rough. Blossom always wore an old shawl on these occasions, held with a cairngorm brooch on the shoulder. Lucille, less fastidious, dirtied whatever clothes she was wearing at the time. If the weather was hot, very hot, she told him, she and the boys stripped off. Blossom didn't. He had never seen Blossom totally naked. Stu, he imagined, had.

With the buskers away, he had to do the cooking. He had suggested to Frances that she might like to help. She had ignored the suggestion and would have ignored the food, too, if he hadn't insisted that she should eat something.

Quinn felt it was about time they had a conversation about her father, but he kept putting it off.

She surprised him by raising the subject herself. It was early evening and he had gone to the greenhouse to give the orchids another drink. Frances, made thirsty by association, asked him if he had any lager in the house. He thought it likely. It was Lucille's tipple. He was about to tell her to go and look, but realised that in looking her eyes would alight on the whisky.

He went to look for it himself and when he'd found it called her in.

She took the tumbler from him and drank eagerly. 'Tomorrow,' she said, 'I'd like you to take me to Wales.'

He had poured himself a lager, too, and drank it without enthusiasm. 'Why?'

'I need to go back to where it happened.' Her voice was flat and emotionless.

He felt his way cautiously. 'Wales is more than a ten-minute spin in the country. I have to be in court Monday morning.'

She went to fiddle with the radio and got a raucous blast of music from a foreign station. 'We could leave early,' she said over the din. 'It's no more than four or five hours. We'll be there by midday and back in the evening.'

Quinn pointed out that there might be a police presence in the area to keep sightseers away.

'Sightseers? In that remote place? Oh, no— not there.'

He thought she was probably right about this. A gutted cottage somewhere in the wilds didn't rate the same interest as Carne's London home. He agreed to take her. For the first time she was being positive, but whether for better or worse, he didn't know.

They left just before eight the next morning. He heard her moving about downstairs at half past seven and hoped she was cooking breakfast.

She wasn't, but had cut some sandwiches. 'We can't stop anywhere public to eat,' she told him, 'we might be recognised.' She had found a flask and was putting coffee in it. Lager last night. Coffee this morning. An improvement all round, thought Quinn.

And then he saw the whisky bottle at the bottom of the basket. He let it stay.

He took the motorway for as far as it went. The sun shone and the wind had abated. A pleasant day for the buskers. He envied them their youth, their freedom, their peace of mind.

They stopped to eat at a layby on a quiet road just north of Shrewsbury. Afterwards she disappeared modestly behind some bushes. He waited until she came back and then went to do the same. When he returned to the car Quinn was pleased to see that she had found some chocolate in the glove-compartment. She needed all her strength for this bloody business. What, he wondered, would poking around in Daddy's murky past reveal? So far he had asked her nothing and they had spoken very little. The car radio, like a third person babbling in the background, took the discomfort out of non-communication.

The final part of the drive was into the stark beauty of the mountains softened on the lower slopes by heather and gorse. The air smelt as if it had blown in from distant seas. It was a good place.

A good place for murder?

Frances had rolled down her window and was leaning her arm along it. A thin arm, speckled with freckles. The sun was slanting across her face and her eyes were half-closed. Battered by sunlight, not soothed. He told her she'd find sunglasses where she'd found the chocolate. She said she didn't need them, that they wouldn't fit over her own glasses. He told her she didn't need those either, that tinted glass which didn't magnify was an affectation. She answered that her father had said the same thing. The response had come quickly and she had spoken his name without emotion.

After the next half-dozen miles she started directing him. She was sitting lower in the seat now and gazing out furtively like a prisoner on the run. He suggested sarcastically that she might like to drape a blanket over her head in case the villagers saw her.

'Is that what he does in the prison van?'

He mentally apologised for an ill-considered remark. 'He' now, not 'father'. Bitterness in the voice. A regression.

He answered honestly. 'No. He looks as calm as if he's leaving Broadcasting House. Still gets the odd cheer from the crowd, too.'

'His loving fans.' Very bitter.

He changed the subject. 'Do we drive through the village of Brynglas?'

'No. We turn left at the next side road—it's

158

coming up now—and do a loop. In about three or four minutes be ready to stop.'

'We'll be at the cottage?' He was surprised. 'I thought it was up a track?'

'It is. We'll be near the craft centre. But not too near.' She told him to turn the car into a farm gateway. 'It's rarely used. We're not likely to block a tractor or anything.'

He realised with surprise that she knew the area very well. Olivia Mason had given the impression that she hardly knew her. One brief meeting in the village. Perhaps Olivia had been lying.

'You visited the Masons sometimes?'

Her face was averted and he barely heard her answer, 'Now and then.'

They walked across a field, keeping to the path, and then she turned left and ascended a gently rising hill. Quinn, though not a countryman, was aware that they were walking over young green shoots and probably shouldn't be. He couldn't put a name to them. There was no farm in sight. He followed her. At the top of the hill hedges were allowed to grow high to form a wind-break.

She stopped. 'That's it.'

Two fields away there was a minor road and on it with no front garden was a long low building comprising two converted cottages with the third that formed the row left in its original state. One of the front windows had

159

been enlarged to display some of the crafts on sale, but from this distance it wasn't possible to see any of the items clearly. What had once been an inn sign was fixed over the shop area; the words 'Country Crafts' were painted on it in white letters on a black background. To the side of the building and encroaching into the field behind was a pebbled area that would hold about a dozen cars. An old-fashioned buggy was parked there. It was varnished and looked very clean.

'David's work,' Frances said.

'David?'

'Olivia's husband.'

Olivia's husband who had been having an argument with Jocelyn Carne—and was now dead. Olivia Mason had told the prosecuting counsel that he had died of a heart attack. The innkeeper had said that she had nursed him well.

Quinn decided that it was time to probe.

'Tell me about him.'

'Tell you *what?*' She was emotional, edgy.

'Anything relevant—mainly why it upsets you when I ask you to tell me.'

She broke off a tendril of honeysuckle from the hedge and shredded the petals through her fingers.

'He died in January. He was thirty-two. He made solid, honest-looking things. He had a hell of a marriage. I'm not upset.'

Thirty-two years old. He had imagined him older—a frail middle-aged man. At thirty-two he was young enough to be attractive to Frances—and not too young to be attractive to her mother.

A hell of a marriage. Why?

He asked it. 'Didn't they get on?' It was a pallid way of putting it.

She didn't answer.

He put it to her differently. 'The innkeeper spoke highly of both of them. He made a point of expressing the villagers' view of them as a couple. I believe he used the word "respected".'

'Oh, Bowen of the Mitre gave evidence, did he?'

Not everything had been reported. There were large areas of evidence of which she knew nothing. 'As I remember, he stressed that she was an excellent wife.'

She smiled thinly. 'Go on—tell me more.'

'Olivia Mason gave the impression that she knew your father and mother in a neighbourly sort of way. She said her husband did some minor repairs at the cottage.'

'Then she's a genius at understatement,' Frances retorted sharply. 'David could turn a lump of wood into anything and make it beautiful. He was a craftsman. All she can do is turn out material the colour of cat's shit.'

He was learning. The talented David, now dead, was growing at the edge of his

161

imagination. Was he the catalyst that had caused the final explosion?

He told her about her mother's meeting with him in the Mitre a few days before the fire. 'According to Bowen, there was an argument.'

She closed in on herself and turned away from him.

He pressed on. 'What was the argument about?'

She humped her thin shoulders into a shrug. 'How should I know?'

'About you, perhaps? He seems to have impressed you. Did you ever sleep with him?'

'Mind your own bloody business.' But it wasn't emphatic. If he had touched a nerve, he hadn't jabbed it.

He wondered if his next question would. 'The prosecuting counsel asked Olivia Mason what her husband's relationship was with your mother.'

Frances took a few paces away from him and sat on the grass. She kicked off her shoes and leaned back on her elbows. Clouds were cobwebbing across the sky. A bee ravaged a buttercup. She dug her fingers into the soil and rimmed her scarlet fingernails with black. She kept her head averted.

Quinn knew that there would be no answer unless he forced one. 'She implied that there was nothing between them. Was she lying?'

Frances stayed silent.

He persisted. 'There are several permutations. One: your mother and David Mason were lovers. Two: you and David Mason were lovers. Three: Olivia Mason and your father were lovers. In a sane world none of it adds up to murder, but we're not all of us sane all the time. Am I getting anywhere near the truth?'

She surprised him by grinning suddenly with almost manic amusement. 'Jesus! Even if David and I had gone to bed together, why should anyone murder my mother?'

She was looking at him through half-closed eyes, a long, considering, somehow challenging stare. Briefly and disconcertingly, she had distanced herself from him.

He squatted on the grass beside her. 'All right, I agree. Let's look at the more likely one. Your mother and David Mason. Your father—or even Olivia—or perhaps both together—killed her.' He was being brutally inquisitorial, but he needed to know.

She was no longer smiling. 'Why should a man like David be attracted to a woman in her forties?'

He thought briefly of Selina McKay who was even more sexually desirable in her maturity than his beautiful Blossom. 'It happens. It could have happened. Did it?'

'No.' A flat denial. He believed her.

'Then we're left with the third permutation.

163

Your father and Olivia Mason. An argument. Tempers lost. Your mother refusing a divorce, perhaps. Murder in a mad moment—most of them are—an impulsive killing. Was that it?'

He had an uncanny feeling that he was homing in on something, but that the target was slightly out of true.

Her face looked bruised, older. She got up suddenly and pushed her feet into her shoes. 'What about Hester Allendale?' she asked bitterly. 'Doesn't she come into your permutations anywhere? How about bedding her down with David? That would make a change, wouldn't it? An up-dated *La Ronde*. Pity you weren't around at the time to join in.'

She started back down the field. He caught up with her on the path. 'In a day or two, the jury retires. I shouldn't be one of them. If I'm to continue breaking the rules, I need to have a valid reason—such as knowing the truth.'

She looked at him bleakly and went on walking.

He took her arm and made her stand still.

'I came here to think,' she said. 'You keep thrusting stupid ideas at me and pressing me for answers. Give me time. Give me until the end of the day. I might have something to tell you then.'

He had to be satisfied with that.

When they returned to the car she said she wanted to be driven to the cottage. He knew it

164

would be traumatic for her, but agreed. The rutted track was hard and dry. Carne's Granada, according to the evidence, was muddy. It had been a grey wet evening, perhaps, and yet the fire had blazed.

Around them the hills crept up into the mountains. Grass gave way to slate-grey stones slashed with black where the sun failed to penetrate, and a pale silver-yellow where it shone. A place of contrasts. Sombre as a cathedral. Beautiful but cold.

The remains of the cottage, like charred bones, lay in a hollow. Here and there nature had pushed up clumps of dandelions which glowed like miniature flames. A chimney pot, keeled over on its side, was full of twigs and moss—a half-finished nest.

She was walking ahead of him, her feet scuffing up dusty soil impregnated with ash. He leaned against what was once the garden wall and watched her. He guessed that she was entering rooms that were no longer there. A few paces to the right. A hallway? A few more paces onwards. A kitchen? A living-room? A bedroom? He wondered where it had happened. Jocelyn Carne had been reclining. In bed or on a chair?

Blood had been found by the back door. Was that where she was walking now? Her footsteps were slow and heavy and her body was bent over in a slouch. Suddenly she was slumping forward on her knees, almost as if she were praying—or about to pass out?

He went over to her swiftly. Her face was ashen like the ground under her and her eyes were glazed. She was beginning to sway. He knelt beside her and held her around the shoulders, supporting her. 'You'll be all right,' he said gently. 'Just take it easy—take it steady—you're okay.' Trite words, but the only ones that came to him. She wasn't okay. She was in the middle of an appalling crisis. It would be more therapeutic to tell her to scream, to batter the ground with her fists.

Her colour came back slowly and she was less of a weight against him. When she was capable of moving, he helped her to her feet and walked her back to the car. He poured whisky into the plastic cup of the Thermos flask and helped steady her hand while she drank it.

It was some time before she was ready to speak. When she did, it was to tell him that she wanted to go home.

Home? Her own home? Had she come to some decision back there?

'You want to go back to your own home?'

She looked at him in surprise. 'No,' she said, 'yours.'

Had he hammered her with questions on the drive back while she was at too low an ebb to resist, he might have found the truth. It was something he couldn't do. She sat with her eyes closed, not sleeping but totally withdrawn.

They arrived home at seven. Home. He turned the word over in his mind. This tall, gloomy, decaying house—home? Was that really the way she saw it?

She stood in the hall and shivered. 'It's cold.'

It was a mild summer evening, but he could see that she was trembling. 'I'll light a fire in the living-room.'

'Not for me. I'm going to bed.'

He told her it was early. 'I'll cook us something. Go after you've eaten if you must.' He took the picnic basket through to the living-room and put it down on the table.

She followed him. 'You keep pushing food at me. I don't want it.'

'Please yourself. I do. I'll get the fire going first.'

The fire was already laid. She watched as he put a match to it. He could have switched on the electric heater; it wasn't a ruse, just a thoughtless action that worked.

'There were several gallons of petrol in the shed,' she said. 'I think my mother must have hoarded it during a period of shortage.' She spoke in a normal voice. No stress.

'Oh, yes?' He didn't turn around, but eased pieces of coal carefully over the firewood. It was the original Edwardian grate with chipped yellow and green flower tiles down the sides. He was staring intently at them without really

167

seeing them, all his senses alert to what she was telling him.

'It was a damp night,' she went on, 'but there was a wind. It helped the cottage to blaze.'

'You saw it?' It had occurred to him uneasily more than once that she might have been there.

'No, my father told me.'

He kept looking at the grate, not at her. Relief that she had no part in it flooded him.

The silence was broken by a piece of coal falling on to the hearth.

'My father,' she said, 'was a bastard to my mother. He flaunted his women in front of her. He crippled her with neglect. He made her what she became.'

What she became? What was she trying to tell him? He waited, afraid to look at her or move in case he snapped the thin thread of communication.

When she spoke again her voice was less controlled. 'There's more than one way of killing. His is the worst. The law might say he's not guilty. I don't.'

The law might say he's not guilty. A declaration of her father's innocence? *I don't.* Meaning the law—the jury—might get it wrong and so put Carne away for life?

He picked up the fallen piece of coal with the tongs and placed it back in the fire. He sensed she had more to tell him and was finding it difficult. He turned and looked at her. She looked back at him. The eye contact was abrasive.

And then she turned away and went over to the picnic basket on the table. She began unpacking it, standing with her back to him.

'You asked me if I went to bed with David. I didn't.' She put the empty sandwich bag next to the empty flask. 'He attracted me, but it didn't happen.' She made a silver ball of the chocolate paper and put it neatly into the cup of the flask. 'We were alone here last night—and again tonight—but you don't make a pass at me.' She turned slowly on her heel and faced him. 'What's wrong with me?'

The question took him by surprise, but he sensed that it was relevant and that the answer was important. She was unsure of herself sexually. She needed reassurance. If he took her to bed now there would be tenderness but no loving spontaneity. It might be a fiasco. She needed to learn, with someone younger, when her world was normal again and not as it was now, falling apart.

'While you're in my care,' he said, 'we don't.'

'The honourable Robert Quinn,' it was deeply sarcastic. 'If you're looking for a cop out—then be honest. I think you sleep alone. You're not gay—so why?'

He decided to answer with a half-truth. 'I sleep alone when Blossom isn't around. The fact that she's away doesn't alter anything.'

She looked at him in disbelief. 'Blossom? That little Chinese? Christ!' It was derisive.

Under different circumstances he might have been angry. Blossom had been good to her.

He tried to turn the conversation back to Carne again. 'Have you anything else to tell me about your father? Can't you tell me more clearly what you're trying to say?'

She took the whisky bottle out of the basket. 'I'm taking this upstairs. Don't try to stop me. I need it. I don't think I'll sleep. If you want to come to me—then come.'

'Frances, you haven't answered me.'

'Nor will I. He told me to say nothing. I've said too much.'

She was beginning to cry and her face, so like her mother's, became mottled and ugly. She put her arm across it in a childish gesture to hide it. He felt her pain, sharp inside himself, but resisted following her when she left the room and went upstairs.

During the night her words kept battering at him. 'The law might say he's not guilty.' Not 'The *jury* might say' which would be ambiguous. The *law*. It was an important difference. Unequivocal. It could be a statement of her father's innocence.

He made up his mind to smash the question at her in the morning. To hell with gentleness. Her hurt was of less importance now than her father's need.

But when he went downstairs shortly after seven, he realised he was too late. She had left him a note. It was scrawled with a water-soluble pen on the kitchen reminder board under Blossom's grocery list and propped up against the coffee percolator.

When you read this I'll have gone out. I don't want to talk to you. I won't come back until you've left for the Old Bailey. If the jury retires today, then do what you can for him.

There was one permutation you didn't think of. My mother and Olivia Mason were lovers. Grotesque, isn't it!

I think what you told me about Blossom is a lot of crap. Why didn't you come to me last night? I think I could love you.

It ended there. Abruptly.

CHAPTER ELEVEN

Edward Carne had spent an excellent night, sleeping deeply and awakening refreshed. He was quite happy not to go into the witness-box. Let the prosecution and defence hammer it out between them as best they could. On arriving at court this morning he had smiled cheerfully at everyone. It was a beautiful summer day. Nice for his fans. And his enemies. The barracking as his van drew up hadn't bothered him. He resented no one. Not even the jury. That his calm would be shattered at some later stage didn't worry him now. Let them do their worst. It didn't matter.

If this were being mad then it was a soothing form of madness. How had Socrates reacted, he wondered, when he had been given the hemlock? Had he been curious about the taste? Had the cup felt cold against his tongue? Had he been afraid or had his imagination been neatly tethered—as his was neatly tethered?

A life sentence was a death sentence prolonged. He no longer sweated over the fact. He couldn't see it in his mind. His brain built no bogeys to taunt him. Inside his head everything was under control. Jocelyn moved along the edge of his thoughts, but greyly, and without form.

It was easy to concentrate on the unimportant. He had run out of toothpaste this morning and been given a new tube. It wasn't his usual brand. Rather better, in fact. Minty and refreshing. He ran his tongue over his teeth and tried to recollect the taste.

Hester Allendale, in the days before her stage success, had done a toothpaste commercial. Sexy voice. Sexy smile. A lovely anonymous lady. She was in court today dressed in dark red. He undressed her in his mind and felt neither excitement nor desire. She *knew* he had killed Jocelyn, she had stated. Well, clever she. He wished she would turn around and look at him, but she kept her head averted.

McNair had mentioned her during the conference he and the solicitor had with him at Brixton on Saturday evening. 'The vicious evidence of an attractive actress,' he'd pointed out, 'makes more of an impression that that of the dull but well-meaning character witnesses.'

Richardson, who had been sitting in comparative silence until then, had agreed. 'You need a witness who'll do you some positive good. An honest statement of where you were on the night would give the defence some kind of foundation. As it is, it's as weak as a house of cards.'

The remark, though true, was tactless. McNair had ignored it. Better a weak house of cards, his quick glance at Carne had implied, than a defence blasted by the truth.

Later, just before leaving, McNair had rephrased the solicitor's words so that Carne could give him the answer he wanted. 'Your refusal to provide an alibi has done you considerable harm,' he said quietly, 'but it isn't too late to help yourself—even now. If you can come up with a name—a place—anything that proves you weren't in the cottage—then tell me. If you can't . . .' Deliberately he hadn't finished the sentence.

'Sorry,' Carne had said, 'just do the best you can.'

McNair's best would need to be good, Carne realised, as he listened to Breddon's closing speech. The counsel for the prosecution was addressing the jury in crisp, clear sentences like a headmaster preparing examinees. They were to clear their minds of prejudice, he was telling them, and look coolly at the evidence. He began listing it.

Carne had been seen in the vicinity on the night of the murder. He had bought tyres at a nearby garage to replace ones that were on the Granada. The four original tyres were almost new, but he had disposed of them. Was he anticipating that the police would have tyre prints of the car at the cottage? Was it a calculated act?

He reminded the jury of the pathologist's evidence and described the brutal way in which Jocelyn had been killed. 'I must point out to you that no blood-stained clothing belonging to the accused was found during the police search of his premises. But this search occurred four months after the murder. There was ample time to destroy the clothing—as the tyres were destroyed.'

He went on to speak of the anonymous phone call. 'If the woman hadn't told the police about the location of Jocelyn's body, it's extremely unlikely it would have ever been discovered.

174

Her murderer would have gone free. If she hadn't directly accused Carne the evidence relating to his presence in the area wouldn't have come to light.' He spoke with heavy emphasis, 'If Carne had admitted to being in the area and given a good reason for being there— and *refuted* the accusation—it might be possible to believe in his innocence. He has chosen to remain silent.

'You may wonder who this woman is and to what degree she is involved in the crime. An accessory? An unwilling witness? If the latter, she should have reported the crime immediately. If the former, one understands her long silence—without, of course, condoning it. She remained silent for four months and then, for reasons we can only guess at—extreme anger with Carne—jealousy, perhaps—she "shopped" him. You will, I hope, forgive the colloquialism. It is more apt, in this instance, than the word "betray".'

Breddon folded his arms and looked thoughtfully at the jury for a couple of minutes before continuing.

'And now we come to the motive for the murder. We're not on solid ground here. I can't tell you that it was for this reason—or for that— but I can remind you of the evidence of some of the witnesses. Carne, you will recall, had more than one lover. His relationships were, at times, tempestuous. You will remember Hester

Allendale's evidence. Carne was the father of the child she had aborted. We don't know his feelings about this. We do know his marriage was in decline. It's possible he wanted his freedom and his wife refused it. Emotions might have been running high for some time. There could have been a quarrel, probably one of many, but this time blows are struck. Tragically, it all goes too far. It's the simple explanation and the most likely one.'

Carne, listening to Breddon's grating voice, thought: tragic—yes; simple—no. Tragedy was synonymous with pain, but he continued to feel nothing.

'The ordinary domestic murder happens all too frequently,' Breddon went on. 'It's a sad fact of life. A crime of passion cannot be condoned, but it can be understood. It becomes totally heinous when there is concealment. To bury the body and then cold-bloodedly act out the charade of searching for it is behaviour most damnable.

'Remember, too, the fire. An excellent and very thorough fire, but not quite thorough enough to destroy the blood stains by the back door. Jocelyn Carne was killed in the cottage. She wasn't murdered by a stranger on a lonely mountain track and then hastily buried. She was murdered in her own home. She was driven in her own car up the mountain track and then carried the remainer of the way and concealed in a hole in the heather. Her car and the cottage were then set alight. Do you seriously believe that a homicidal maniac in the guise of a mountain climber or a hiker would go to all that trouble?' He smiled derisively.

'This is a very simple and clear-cut case. You should have no difficulty in arriving at the verdict. I submit that Edward Carne murdered his wife, Jocelyn. In her prime of life she was brutally done to death by him. Afterwards, Carne continued to shine forth in his *Arcadia* programmes—a priest of humbug in a landscape of innocence. Good, clean country entertainment hosted by an evil man with no conscience and no compassion. Judge him for what he is.'

★   ★   ★

McNair's speech for the defence struck a more emotional note. Carne, a victim of circumstances, wrongly accused. He dwelt on the lack of evidence against him and pointed out that the murder weapon hadn't been found. 'If it had been discovered on Carne's premises he would have had a case to answer.' He told the jury to consider the lack of motive. 'Carne's extra-marital adventures had been going on for some time. Had he wished to marry one of his mistresses, and his wife wasn't willing to divorce him, do you seriously believe that in this modern age he would have removed the obstacle to his bliss by murdering her? Surely he would have just moved in with the new woman in his life and made her his common-law wife.'

He implored the jury to scrutinise every aspect of the case without bias, to discount the chimera, and to come to the obvious conclusion of his client's innocence. 'You cannot condemn a man because he buys new tyres for his car. It is quite impossible to prove that they were bought with a sinister motive. As to the accusation made by the anonymous telephone caller, you must treat that with the contempt it deserves. There is no supporting evidence linking Carne with the crime. The caller knew the whereabouts of the body. He could have been the murderer. We have no voice prints to prove that the telephone call was made by a woman. There is a great deal about this case, ladies and gentlemen, that remains closed to us—including the private life of Jocelyn Carne. Why, do you suppose, did she find that remote cottage so attractive? Was she having an affair with someone in the area? She was a woman in early middle age—young enough to form a loving relationship with another man. A relationship that might have soured and ended in violence. Is it too difficult to believe that her lover killed her and then several months later accused Carne of the killing? We walk an uneasy road, members of the jury, if the mantle of guilt can be swung so easily over the shoulders of the innocent.'

He spoke for just over an hour. It was a valiant and at times quite plausible effort.

At twelve-thirty the court rose. Mr Justice Spencer-Leigh's summing up would take place in the afternoon, and the jury would then retire to consider their verdict. He told them that it was advisable that they should lunch in the Old Bailey restaurant to avoid contact with the crowds outside.

Quinn, not heeding the advice, found a restaurant he hadn't eaten at before. He ordered Coke and roast-beef sandwiches and closed his mind to the conversation around him. McNair's guess about Jocelyn having a lover had been right—but he'd got the sex wrong.

He remembered Frances' word on the note: *grotesque.*

Before coming to court he had walked the streets for nearly an hour looking for her. A last-minute plea to do what he could for her father wasn't good enough. If it was her way of saying he was innocent, then the declaration had been venomously delayed. Her mother's lesbianism had shocked her into unfair hatred of her father. Her attitude was unrealistic. Lesbians were born, not made. Carne's consolation in the arms of other women was understandable. Frances had got the sequence the wrong way around. Had she told him all this at the beginning he would have persuaded her to go home and give evidence on her father's behalf.

But what evidence?

If Jocelyn had threatened to leave Carne for Olivia wasn't his anger likely to be greater than if she had threatened to leave him for another man? An unnatural situation, but surely acceptable in these tolerant days when sexual aberrations were looked on with some sympathy. Not worthy of murder.

Unless he'd caught them in the act, perhaps, and lost his cool. But wouldn't Olivia have gone directly to the police if her lover was murdered in front of her?

Unless her husband had done the murder.

Had Olivia kept quiet during her husband's lifetime and then phoned the police anonymously after he had died? But instead of blaming her husband she had blamed Carne. If so, by what twisted logic had she come to the conclusion that Carne should shoulder the guilt? Did her mind work like Frances's? A belief that Carne's attitude to Jocelyn had caused a slow dying during an unhappy marriage and was more reprehensible than the violent ending of it? Or was she simply being protective of her husband's memory?

If so, why didn't Carne accuse him? Because he was an accessory, perhaps, and thought it safer to deny all involvement.

Or Frances could have killed her mother. She had implied, not stated, that she wasn't there.

Her father had told her about the fire, she said. She could have been lying. He didn't believe she was. She had touched her mother's photograph in the paper with tenderness, and surely if there had been guilt she couldn't have borne to look at it? Her emotions were extreme, at times almost paranoid, but all her anger was directed at her father. It had taken a great deal of hatred to allow him to stand in the dock if she believed in his innocence. A last-minute change of heart, if that's what it was, was leaving it bloody late.

Once Carne was sent down, probably for life, it would be difficult to resurrect the case. He could stop the trial now by declaring involvement. He could speak to Carne's defence counsel and tell him what Frances had told him. Only she hadn't told him very much—nothing that would carry weight. A daughter panicking at the prospect of life imprisonment for her father—that's the way most people would see it.

So why put his own head on the block and be arraigned for contempt of court when it would be so much easier to battle with the rest of the jurors for an acquittal?

But why battle at all? Why not let 'justice' take its course? Because he had sufficient imagination to know what life imprisonment must be like. Because justice too often was a lunatic concept. Butler had summed it up, he couldn't remember where:

181

Justice gives sentence many times,
On one man for another's crimes.

Carne might have killed his wife, not proven, but incarcerate him anyway. It wasn't good enough.

So get him off.

But if he failed?

But why think of failure? There were several hours of argument before the end of the day. In the meantime Spencer-Leigh would, no doubt, show his own personal bias. He wondered what form the judge's direction would take.

★　　★　　★

Spencer-Leigh's summing-up ran a careful middle course. He had a dry, rather pedantic voice and placed emphasis on certain key words.

He began with a review of the evidence, stressing that for the most part it was circumstantial. 'In many murder trials, members of the jury, a verdict of guilty has been correctly returned on circumstantial evidence alone. Murder by its very nature is a private act, carefully concealed. But circumstantial evidence must be strong enough to exclude all reasonable alternatives—it must prove the case beyond all reasonable doubt.' He paused, giving the jury time to understand the importance of what he was saying.

'Now, in the trial of Edward Carne we have an anonymous accuser. It would have been direct evidence if whoever made the phone call had stood in the witness-box and given details of the crime as a credible eye-witness. Anonymity is less than satisfactory.' Here, the judge reminded the jury of McNair's and Breddon's opposing theories regarding the sex and motive of the caller. 'It is up to you to give these theories whatever credence you think they merit. There is one incontrovertible fact, however: the body was where the caller said it was. The question for you to answer in the course of your deliberations is: did Carne put it there?'

He checked his notes before speaking again. 'In the words of his producer, Carne was a dedicated professional who wouldn't leave his unfinished work during the filming in Devon without an urgent reason. Carne gave him no explanation. He left hurriedly and drove north. This was the third of August. On the morning of the fourth of August he was at Weston's garage, a few miles from the cottage, and on his way back to London. By this time the cottage was gutted and Jocelyn was dead. What happened during the crucial hours before he made the return journey is up to you to decide. Had he been on the premises—and been innocent—would he have driven away and not reported her death? Or could he have visited the cottage earlier, and left before the murder? When he searched for his wife's body, was he aware all the time where it was? Or did he search in all innocence? Why was he accused of his wife's murder by the anonymous caller if he had no hand in it? Why didn't he go into the witness-box and deny the accusation? These are questions for you to think about.'

He looked briefly at Carne before continuing. 'There is an important point that the defence counsel brought to your notice—no murder weapon has been traced to Carne. If one had been, your task would be easier. There is no tangible proof to assist you—one way or the other. As for the absence of blood-stained clothing—is it likely, do you think, that Carne would have stopped at the garage if his clothing had been blood-stained?

'With regard to the tyres: defence counsel has pointed out that they were probably bought with no ulterior motive—this could well be so. If it is the case, then it is unfortunate for Carne that the original tyres were not left on the car, or produced during the search of his premises. They could have proved that his car was not parked on the track by the cottage on the night of the murder.

'Now we come to the question of motive.' He shook his head and pursed his lips. 'Human nature is an imponderable. It is impossible to know how Carne might react to certain situations. A great deal has been spoken from the witness-box about his character, and I refer specifically to the testimony of Miss Allendale. Her emotional outburst accusing him of the crime shouldn't be taken too seriously. The anonymous phone call is a different matter. You must consider that very seriously, indeed.'

He went over the salient points of the case once more, and ended with a solemn instruction: 'It is for you to judge the facts in the light of everything you have heard during the course of the trial. Remember that Carne's guilt has to be proved to your complete satisfaction before you can return a verdict of guilty. A verdict of not guilty requires no such proof. You must endeavour to reach a unanimous verdict. Bear in mind during your deliberations that whatever conclusion you come to you are not wielding judicial power over the defendant. The consequences of the verdict must not trouble your consciences. I must now ask you to retire to the jury room and consider very carefully and dispassionately all the evidence at your disposal.'

Carne, still very composed, had listened intently to the judge's summing-up. Now, for the first time for days, he let his eyes roam over the jury—one by one. They were a motley lot. Some too old. Some too young. He wondered what they thought of him but wasn't greatly bothered. Your busy minds, he thought, worrying away at scraps of information—most of it wrong.

THE VERDICT

CHAPTER TWELVE

Shortly before three o'clock the jury bailiff took the oath: 'I swear that I will keep this jury in some private and convenient place. I shall not suffer anyone to speak to them neither will I speak to them myself without leave of the court, unless it be to ask them whether they have agreed upon their verdict. So help me God.'

For the first few minutes after the bailiff had escorted them to the jury room, the jurors stood on the threshold like travellers surveying an inimical island. Being cast upon it was the inevitable outcome of the journey. Over the past week most of them had tried to envisage the scene. It was more or less what they had expected, but reality had the cold edge on imagination. This, disturbingly, was it. Some wished they could turn around and go out again—just freely depart. Was the door locked? They noticed with relief the adjoining lavatory.

There was a large central table with chairs neatly arranged around it. The table dominated the room. Quinn, looking at it, suddenly remembered appalling dinner parties in the days of his affluent youth when the guests had been even more ill-assorted than this lot. Professor

Leary was reminded of university committee meetings, and immediately decided to take charge of this one. There would have to be a foreman and he didn't see anyone else measuring up to it. There was a chair at the head of the table. He took it.

'My tall friend,' Quinn said, indicating Jacobson, 'needs leg-room. I suggest you relinquish that chair to him.'

Jacobson, deeply embarrassed, said that he had no wish for the chair of honour, just a position at the table that wasn't too confined.

'There is no chair of honour,' Quinn pointed out. 'The foreman is just the mouthpiece of all of us. As yet we haven't got one. For God's sake, man, sit where you're comfortable.'

Leary rose, 'Of course.'

Jacobson sat down and smiled evilly like a bouncer who had just ejected an unruly customer. That the smile was conciliatory no one could guess. He felt extremely ill at ease. During the period of the trial he had been living in a climate of violence, glad to escape each evening to the company of his wife and daughters. He felt no affinity with his fellow jurors. That they must eventually be of one mind worried him. Carne, he had no doubt at all, had murdered his wife. It was an appalling crime to batter to death the woman who bore your children. Or, in this case, one absent daughter. If his own daughters turned their backs on him for any reason he wouldn't want to go on living.

'At least he won't hang,' Peter Lomax said, taking a seat half-way along the table. 'I saw a public execution on one of my carpet-buying trips to the Middle East. I didn't mean to, just got carried along with the crowd. It was a decapitation. Very bloody. Shooting is worse, of course. There isn't the same accuracy. And hanging is the worst of the lot.' He was talking very fast and very nervously. Some of the older women were looking shocked. Well, damn it, it was brass-tacks time now. They weren't about to sit around a table and be given afternoon tea in the best china while the local vicar discussed parish affairs. He wondered who would take on the role of foreman. If it was offered to him he would refuse it.

'Disgusting man,' Irene Sinclair whispered to Selina McKay. If you got carried along with the crowd you fought for an exit, and if you couldn't find one you gritted your teeth and closed your eyes. Or you opened them and yelled 'stop'. You didn't bring your terrible memories into a room where an irrevocable decision had to be taken and talk about them. She wished she could feel calmer, less emotional. Until today she had been stimulated by the trial. There had been something of interest to tell her sister when she went home. Cornwallis had been useful, too, with his plans for the new bathroom. And his records of bird-song which Cleo liked to listen to. She had been grateful to Carne for opening out her horizon a little. That she should now be called upon to obliterate his horizon—or to let him wander freely into the far-off yonder and perhaps kill again—was too heavy a responsibility. She didn't feel equal to it and began physically to ache.

Selina, not knowing whether she was intended to hear the remark or not, ignored it. Her mind was in a state of chaos. Her husband had phoned the previous evening to say that he was staying on in Brussels for an extra few days. He had met a colleague at the medical conference who had been at Bart's with him and had persuaded him to make a social occasion of it. If she hadn't been tied up with jury duty, Haydon had said, she could have flown over and joined them. The hotel was excellent. In the course of conversation it had turned out that the colleague was a woman, Clare something-or-other. A purely professional relationship, Haydon had been careful to make clear. Now, looking across the table at Quinn, Selina chose not to believe him. It was very pleasant not to be appalled—not even mildly worried. Her conscience, carefuly caged for years, fluttered hopefully against the bars.

'An unpleasant experience for you,' Quinn answered Lomax, 'but speedy for the victim. Have you ever imagined what it's like to slop out urine every day of your life?'

Everyone was sitting now. He was next to Professor Leary and could feel the man's dislike of him crackle out of him like electricity. Leary again remembered the demise of his cat. He could cheerfully have hanged Quinn for it.

'You uphold the death penalty?' he asked suavely.

Quinn didn't. He upheld freedom. Freedom to live or to die. The guilty should be allowed the choice. An argument on the ethics of judicial punishment was unwise, however, especially as he hoped to get Carne acquitted.

'Punishment,' he said, 'of any kind, presupposes guilt. We've only been in this room a matter of minutes. We're here to weigh up the evidence, not jump to untenable conclusions.'

'A verdict of guilty is not necessarily untenable,' Leary answered, 'but I agree it would be grossly unfair to arrive at any conclusion without deep and serious thought.' His gaze flitted over the faces of all the jury members, with the exception of Quinn's which he was careful to ignore. It was a professorial trick. Eyes met hypnotically with eyes and demanded attention. These people were like a herd of sheep on a hillside: they needed to be whistled into line.

He tried again. 'We need a foreman. As Mr Quinn pointed out, a foreman is a spokesman. But he—or she—is helpful in other ways, too. I

191

probably don't know any more about the legal side of Carne's case than you do. I've had no experience in the law-courts. But as a professor I've been trained to present arguments and guide discussions. If you'd like my help in this unhappy business, I'll gladly give it.'

'And I,' said Quinn. The years had rolled away and he was back at one of Leary's tutorials. An irresistible urge for mimicry overtook him. 'The academic life,' he said ponderously, 'can hardly be held as a mirror to the raw reality of what we have heard in court. In my years as a reporter I saw life as it is lived. I was trained to record what I saw. *The Times* made me redundant for reasons of financial exigency, but the knowledge I gleaned there is of continuing practical use. Ladies and gentlemen, I'm at your service if you so wish.'

Selina giggled.

Quinn's mouth curved down solemnly as he looked at her and his eyes sparkled with amusement.

And then he thought of Frances and became serious again. 'Oh, hell,' he said, 'vote on it, why don't you? It doesn't make any odds who does the job, but if we keep arguing the toss we'll get nowhere fast.'

It was perhaps his sardonic take-off of Leary that swung the sympathy of some of the jurors away from him—humour in this situation was unseemly. Or perhaps it was the way he looked.

He had been too busy this morning searching for Frances to bother about his appearance. He might have looked marginally more impressive if he hadn't worn jeans and a checked open-necked shirt. He had shaved sketchily. Blossom cut his hair inexpertly from time to time. It needed cutting again. His voice proclaimed his social niche, which annoyed some, and was something he could do nothing about. It was honed to perfection. Leary's Irish brogue gave his diction a certain classless charm. Today he was dressed formally in a grey suit, a white and grey pinstriped shirt, and a maroon tie. He looked the part.

Colin Middler gave out the paper and pencils which had been placed on a side-table and agreed to count the votes. He gave his own vote to James Cornwallis for no better reason than that they both worked with their hands. Cornwallis repaired bathrooms. He repaired feet.

Cornwallis voted for Irene Sinclair because she had made him welcome in her home and liked his bird-song records. She was a clever woman whom life had somehow thwarted, and being forewoman would be a compensatory prize.

Selina voted for Quinn.

So did Elaine Balfour. She liked him for reasons she couldn't define. It was something to do with his nonconformity, perhaps. He was as invigorating as a whiff of oxygen in rarefied air.

William Dalton gave his vote to the big ape, as he thought of Jacobson. There was something primordial about him. He could imagine him crashing through ancient forests where reptiles festooned the trees and curled in the undergrowth. He was the sort of man who would be kind to his snakes.

Sarah Gayland voted for Quinn to spite Leary. The professor had an air of authority coupled with unctuousness which grated on her her. He reminded her of Trina's father, a nonconformist minister, whom she had met briefly after getting Trina's boy-friend off the premises. He had told both girls to examine their hearts closely, but to be guided by their heads, and had added unflatteringly that the Lord would give wisdom to the ignorant like seed on the barren land. 'He's a caricature,' Sarah told Trina with scant tact, 'all the clerics I know have beards and play the guitar.' 'They're caricatures, too,' Trina had replied sadly, 'they're all caricatures.' She had crossed her fingers surreptitiously as she said it, in case God got back at her. She avoided the men altogether and voted for Irene Sinclair. Her father would approve.

Jacobson, after anxious thought, gave his vote to the professor because he was a professor. He wasn't sure if this was a good reason or not, but Quinn didn't impress him as a suitable alternative. Irene Sinclair gave her vote to him for the same reason. Peter Lomax had been weighing up Quinn's response to his anecdote about the public execution. There had been implied criticism in his tone of voice. Professor Leary had listened in silence. He gave him his vote.

Leary voted for the child, as he thought of Trina Thompson. It would be a vote safely wasted.

Quinn voted for Selina and hoped for her sake that no one else would. He expected Leary to have a large majority and was pleased that the votes had been cast·wildly around and that he and the professor had tied on three votes each.

'As no one has overwhelming faith in either of us,' he said, 'I suggest we scrap the whole silly business and just get on with it.'

Leary wouldn't agree and insisted on a show of hands. This time, he won, eight to four. Quinn's single recruit was Cornwallis. Cornwallis didn't like Quinn, but he liked the professor even less. He wondered if either one or the other had voted for him, but thought it unlikely. He said into the silence before anyone else had a chance to speak, 'It's Edward Carne we're here to think about. Not either of you.' It was aggressive, but heartfelt.

Quinn looked at him approvingly. He seemed a recruit worth having.

Leary wished the jury room had been

equipped with a blackboard. He had occasionally used one in his tutorials. The pros and cons could be conveniently set out with a chalk line down the centre. Here, he had to be content with several sheets of paper and a ballpoint pen for everyone. He suggested to the jurors that they should take two pieces of paper and write *concrete evidence* on one and *circumstantial evidence* on the other.

'That way, ladies and gentlemen, we'll be able to see our way more clearly. To assist you, I'll remind you of what we know to be factual. Perhaps you'd like to number the points as I make them. One: Edward Carne was known to be in the cottage on the night of the murder.'

Known by me, Quinn thought, not by you. And not definitely known by me. Frances had implied he was there. She hadn't stated it.

He decided to dispute it. 'Carne might have been in the cottage. It hasn't been proved. If you insist on writing it down, then it should go under the heading of circumstantial evidence. That's where I'm putting it. I advise the rest of you to do the same.'

Leary's voice was clipped. 'There were two witnesses to his presence.'

'I must contradict you. The vet didn't testify.'

'I'm not referring to the vet. The shepherd saw him and the local baker saw his car parked in a layby near the village. There was a woman with him.'

'The local baker *thought* he saw him. McNair made nonsense of his evidence.'

Leary frowned. Was Quinn fighting him out of bloody-mindedness, he wondered, or did he really believe in Carne's innocence?

Quinn, understanding the unspoken question, was aware that caution was needed. If he were to do Carne any good at all, the jury would have to be persuaded with cool logic—if that were possible. At least he'd have to try. So take it slowly and calmly.

'It's an indisputed fact that Carne was at the garage,' he said. 'A sale was made. His credit card was proof of it. That's what I call hard factual evidence. If you suggest putting that down, then I agree with it.'

'I agree that it should be put down at a later stage,' Leary said. 'But meanwhile I am not prepared to dismiss the evidence of the shepherd and the baker. The shepherd's evidence was emphatic and quite believable. The baker was less definite under cross-examination, but I see no reason to disbelieve him. How did the rest of you react to it?'

The response was hesitant and unclear. Some didn't reply at all.

It would be difficult, Quinn realised, to force eleven other people to list the evidence the way he believed it should be listed—particularly as his belief wasn't firmly based. *The law might say he's not guilty*. Had Frances phrased it that way to be deliberately ambiguous? He wondered if she knew that the jury was out. There might be a news flash on the radio. It would be on the main television news this evening together with the verdict of guilty, unless he could somehow work a miracle. With more control than he knew he possessed he began once again to reason the case for Carne.

At the end of an hour the list of circumstantial evidence had grown, but the factual evidence had advanced by only one point—the phone call accusing Carne.

Quinn did his best to discredit it. 'We all have enemies,' he said reasonably, 'Carne probably more than most. He's in the public eye. A target. Jocelyn Carne is disposed of by murderer unknown. A few months later he makes the phone call implicating Carne. That's McNair's theory. What's so difficult to believe about it?'

Dalton spoke up. 'Carne's silence,' he said briefly. 'He won't go into the witness-box.'

'Silence is sometimes a good thing,' Cornwallis muttered with feeling. 'We don't know his reason. Sometimes it's wise to say nowt.' He had recently been having a running battle with the Inland Revenue over the black economy and was losing. If he'd had any sense, he thought, he wouldn't have declared any of his assets; trying to achieve what looked like a reasonable figure hadn't done him any good.

'Mrs Carne's head was very bloody,' Jacobson

observed sadly. It was the first time he had contributed to the discussion. 'How can a man use his strength to destroy?'

It was a general condemnation of all violence.

'He can and he does,' Professor Leary said abruptly. 'The prosecution has proved to my satisfaction that the man in question is Carne.'

'But not to mine.' Quinn was sweating. He rolled up his shirt sleeves. 'Does anyone mind if I open the window?'

One or two grunted permission. The room was getting claustrophobic. Quinn opened the window at the top. If cooler air came in it wasn't noticeable. He returned to his seat.

'All right—expound your unlikely theory,' Leary invited him. 'A psychopath wanders up to the cottage—take it from there.'

'By using the word "psychopath",' Quinn said, 'you've encapsulated both motive and method. If you read the tabloids you'll know that kind of murder happens all too frequently.'

'Jocelyn Carne was seen in the local pub with Mason,' Lomax recalled. 'They were having an argument. There might be a motive for murder there.'

'What motive?' Leary's voice was repressive. 'You're not suggesting that Mason and Jocelyn Carne were having an affair?'

'It's possible. It could have soured for some reason.'

'A frail aging man with a weak heart—a crime

of violence? Oh, come on!'

'A man in his thirties,' Quinn intervened, 'and perhaps more robust than we're led to believe.' He remembered too late that he wasn't supposed to know any of this.

Leary looked at him sharply and came to the conclusion that he was making it up. He was becoming increasingly certain that Quinn was displaying his personal animosity by taking the opposite point of view. As a student he had been disruptive. In his middle years he was no better.

'Mason is dead,' Middler said. 'If Carne believed he killed his wife, then why not say so?'

'Why, indeed?' Leary agreed. 'If hard factual evidence is thin on the ground, then there's an abundance of circumstantial evidence—all pointing to Carne. He had a close and undisputed involvement with Hester Allendale. That's the love affair we have to look at. The obvious one. She aborted their child. They might have wanted marriage. Jocelyn stood in the way of it. It's a classical case of murder sexually motivated. I think most of you agree with me. It might be a good time to take a vote on it—a show of hands.'

It was too early to vote, but Quinn couldn't stop them. If this was the end of the road for Carne, what would he tell Frances? 'I argued with them for an hour or so—they wouldn't listen'?

'If you're going to take a man's life away,' he

said, 'and that's my interpretation of a life sentence—then you ought to have several good reasons for doing so.' He rephrased it. 'If we're going to condemn him, then let's be sure that what we're doing is right. I'm not sure. At this stage, before I'm convinced otherwise, I don't believe he's been proved guilty. All of you who share my disbelief put your hands up with me.'

He raised his hand. Selina raised hers and so did Elaine Balfour. After some hesitation Trina Thompson did the same. She didn't like being one of a minority but the phrase *Thou must not kill* had jumped into her mind. Her hand wavered as she remembered that Carne wouldn't be executed and that the corpse was Jocelyn Carne. She allowed her hand to remain up because Quinn had seen it and it was too embarrassing to take it down again. She blushed furiously.

Quinn smiled at her.

It was eight to four. The argument would continue.

At five o'clock a court official brought in a trolley with tea, coffee and a choice of sandwiches. The jurors, glad of the break, helped themselves.

Elaine Balfour remembered farm teas at harvest time. Great hunks of home-baked bread and home-cured ham. Hard work. At times satisfying. She had adapted to the environment as best she could. It was, she believed, a wife's duty to adapt. Jocelyn Carne hadn't been much support to her husband when his career had changed his life-style. Hiding away in the cottage had been asking for trouble. Carne, guilty or innocent, deserved some sympathy— so give him the benefit of the doubt—at least for a while.

Selina, doubtful of her own motives when voting for Carne, tried to rationalise them. She was, she knew, deeply influenced by Quinn's belief in his innocence. A belief based on what? Nothing concrete. So why share it? More persuasive arguments had been put forward by Leary. They were not necessarily right. Nothing could be positively proved either way, so why jeopardise a man's freedom? After all, the onus was supposed to be on the prosecution to prove guilt beyond reasonable doubt and she wasn't at all sure that Breddon had done this. Her sympathy wasn't with Jocelyn or with Carne himself. It was like the pendulum of a stopped clock, stuck fast in the middle, but more prone to swing in Carne's favour under Quinn's guiding hand. That the hand should be Quinn's bothered her. She should be able to disassociate herself from him and form her own unbiased conclusions.

Irene Sinclair was having a different crisis of doubt. She had voted with the majority without being fully convinced that she was doing the right thing. How could anyone know what the truth was in this case? Why should she and all these other very ordinary people be thrust into this worrying situation? They weren't mind-readers. Intellectually she saw Carne as a murderer. Emotionally she wanted to believe him innocent. Her life since her retirement had been inhibited by circumstances. She was used to repressing her feelings. Leary's arguments were more coolly analytical than Quinn's and so she went along with them—perhaps wrongly. She wondered how her other co-voters felt and looked at them curiously.

For the most part they had voted guilty and had no qualms about it. The only emotionally motivated guilty verdict was Dalton's. He had to keep reminding himself that Carne's wife hadn't been decapitated, that the head was a model. Even so, the wounds were severe. The shock of seeing them had started off memories that sickened him. He was walking once again through a violent landscape of brutal, mindless murder—and dreaming of it. Last night he had dreamt that one of his reptiles was curling itself around Carne's throat like a hangman's noose. He had felt deep satisfaction at the sight.

★   ★   ★

After the tea break, during which conversation was desultory, it wasn't easy to get back to the business in hand. Cornwallis annoyed everyone by taking out his pipe and stuffing it with strong-smelling tobacco. Sarah Gayland, seated next to him, told him that it made her feel sick. A lot of things, he retorted, made him feel sick, including the snaring of wild-life. Man's inhumanity to man was nothing compared to man's inhumanity to animals. What did she think of vivisection, then? She couldn't care less, she told him. Neither, at the moment, did she care about Carne. 'Your smoke,' she said, 'is killing me.' Better than being battered around the head, he thought crossly; nevertheless he put it out. After a meal he either smoked or slept. As neither was acceptable here, he hoped the deliberations would come to an end soon.

Professor Leary hoped so, too. He told the jury members that they had been out for nearly three hours, surely long enough to reach a decision. 'Let's take it, step by step, from the beginning again. But this time we'll start by examining Carne's personality. A man of ambivalent emotions, wouldn't you say? Ambitious. Unstable. A family man with sexual interests outside the family. You've noticed his attitude in the dock. He could be sitting in a box in the theatre looking at someone else's show.'

Quinn interrupted him. 'If he were mentally unstable there would have been psychiatric evidence from expert witnesses. He's calm because he's innocent.'

'That's your opinion.'

'I'm not the only one holding it.'

Leary hoped that, given time, he would be. He continued his character study of Carne, carefully avoiding undue emphasis. A man with certain personality flaws, under great pressure, might kill. Carne's work carried heavy pressures. A mistress like Hester Allendale wouldn't be easy. There would be emotional storms.

Quinn listened, his eyebrows slightly raised. He was aware that he and Leary were acting out the defence and prosecution of the court-room all over again. Some of the jury were getting bored and irritable.

He suggested during a pause in Leary's rhetoric that the discussion should be opened out more. 'Perhaps if we got away from this table and formed small groups—say three groups of four—we'd be able to talk more freely.'

Leary doubted it, but was wise enough not to argue. When academic groups broke up for discussion they very often ended up swapping racing tips or being vituperative about the lecturer. He said he'd give them half an hour.

'We'll take as long as we need,' Quinn said flatly and in saying so recruited Jacobson. It was one of his favourite sayings when his daughters were practising the piano. 'Take as long as you need,' he'd say, 'to get it *right*.'

'It must be got right,' Jacobson said to Quinn,

205

'absolutely.' He pushed back his chair. 'May I group with you?'

'Delighted,' Quinn said.

By seven o'clock groups had formed and re-formed many times, and Leary called everyone back to the central table for another show of hands. This time Jacobson aligned himself with Quinn whom he'd followed from group to group. Selina, Elaine and Trina remained faithful, which made the voting seven to five. Leary, feeling like a prospective member of parliament at the hustings, managed to hide his ire.

It was Middler who lost his temper. 'God dammit,' he exploded, 'How long does this bloody farce go on?' He looked fiercely at everyone, his face red with rage.

No one answered. Everyone felt some sympathy. The atmosphere in the room was becoming more and more inimical. Jury members that you swopped jokes with during the trial were clamming up with fatigue. Anyone who didn't hold your point of view was mad, or sadistically determined to make you suffer.

Quinn broke the silence. 'Think about Carne thinking about us,' he said quietly. He picked up his pen and looked at Leary. 'And so we carry on?'

CHAPTER THIRTEEN

Carne, after refusing a second game of chess with one of the prison officers, was surreptitiously pricking the flesh of his wrist with a small pin. His flesh was capable of feeling pain. But not much pain. Emotionally he was numb. He stopped the pricking and turned the cuff over so that the bloodstains couldn't be seen. Everyone here was being extremely polite to him. It was like sitting outside an operating theatre, heavily sedated, waiting to be called in. Or waiting for news of a relative already on the table who would either be returned whole or declared dead.

A relative he'd ceased to bother about.

He wished he were reacting more normally. What was the matter with him? Jocelyn, always the stronger partner through all their domestic crises, had shown little or no emotion. She would have approved of him now.

He picked up the early evening newspaper that he had been allowed to read. *Carne jury out* was boldly printed under Stop Press, *verdict expected this evening*. He could have been reading about somebody else for all the interest it aroused in him.

A little after nine, the senior prison officer came to tell him that the jury would be spending the night at a hotel. 'It's always a good sign,' he said cheerfully, 'when they can't agree.'

'Is that so?' said Carne. 'What a consoling thought.' He folded up the newspaper and put it down on the small wooden table. 'So it's back to Brixton?'

The officer's eyes were on his blood-stained wrist. 'Scratched yourself?'

'A pimple,' said Carne.

'If you're offered a sleeping pill tonight,' the officer said, 'then take it. You need a good night's rest.'

Carne told him that for the last few nights he had been sleeping extraordinarily well. He also thanked him politely for his concern. 'You have all been very good to me.'

The prison officer looked at him curiously, at a loss for an answer.

★　　　★　　　★

While Carne was eating a late supper at Brixton—an unappetising pie and chips—the jury members were doing little better at a nearby hotel. The menu consisted of soup, followed by various cold meats and a limp salad. An influx of twelve at short notice was probably the excuse for poor service. The meal was set out in a small private dining-room away from the public area.

'It's the way you get treated on some package

208

holidays,' Cornwallis said to Irene Sinclair who was seated opposite to him. 'They herd you together and give you awful grub. If you go on a special-interest holiday it's usually better. I went on a bird-watching one to the Isle of Skye. That was all right. No complaints.' Irene replied vaguely that she was sure it must be so. She had never been on a package holiday. He asked her if she was worried about her sister being left alone all night. She wasn't. Anticipating that this might happen, she had arranged for a neighbour to be there. One of the Bailey's social workers had phoned home to make sure that the neighbour had arrived. She had.

To be cut off from all contact with the outside world presented difficulties of which the authorities were aware. The jurors who lived alone presented no problems unless they had pets. When Dalton had mentioned his reptiles there had been some consternation. A boa-constrictor, he said, a young one and not fully grown at five feet, was as gentle and companionable as a tame moggy. He had, however, given it ample food before leaving for court in the morning. It would be all right tonight and tomorrow. If this debate began breaking records and went on for weeks, however, the zoo might give it a custodial sentence. His other smaller reptiles should present no feeding problems. They could perhaps be brought to him in the jury room? He wasn't being as jocular as he sounded. Someone soon would find out that he lived in a council flat and his quiet existence with his snakes would be over. If that should happen then Carne was responsible. During the evening's final debate he had urged as hard as he could for a guilty verdict.

Middler, ashamed of his outburst, had put in a mild word or two in support before lapsing into a morose silence. Expecting the trial to be over that day he had booked in several patients for chiropody for the following morning. There would be chaos in the clinic. If he had any doubt about Carne's guilt he would feel less resentment; as it was he had no doubt at all.

Trina Thompson was pleased to be staying at the hotel overnight. It had occurred to her belatedly that bedding her boy-friend down in Sarah's flat was an act of moronic trust. Sarah's plump figure with its well-rounded breasts was dangerously voluptuous. Tomorrow, as soon as her father departed, she would take Ralph home. 'My beloved is mine,' she quoted silently to herself, 'and I am his.' And then, fracturing Solomon's Song by missing out a line or two: 'By night on my bed I sought him whom my soul loveth.' She smiled to herself. Tonight Sarah wouldn't have him.

Sarah's youth hadn't been steeped in church liturgy. She knew no psalms to console her. As the evening had worn on her concern for Carne

210

had grown. The nature of Jocelyn's wounds appalled her and at first she had been convinced of Carne's guilt. But Quinn's robust defence of him in the jury room had rocked her in the other direction. She wasn't sure what she thought. By tomorrow she had to be sure. Her own trespassing on marital property might one day result in her corpse being found in a ditch. She shuddered at the thought. Jocelyn Carne might not have been the paragon she was made out to be, but she hadn't necessarily been killed by her husband. If not by him, then by whom? The old round-about of argument and counter argument began rotating again in her head making it ache and she had an ominous griping in her stomach. She wasn't due for a period for a week and wondered if the hotel bathroom had a vending machine for sanitary towels. From every point of view, life was bloody.

Professor Leary's conversation with Lomax at the dinner table had its bloody aspect, too. They were the last to enter the dining-room and had been given a table for two near the fireplace. The chimney breast was decorated with weapons. Lomax, after inspecting the antique guns and cutlasses with interest, said that he had seen the Moslem Khalifa dance on one of his foreign trips. 'It's very violent. The spectators are asked to feel the edges of the swords. Believe me, they're sharp.'

Leary, who was well travelled, had seen the

211

dance, too. He began expounding on the heroic violence of the Greek legends with particular reference to the exploits of Theseus. 'He murdered most magnificently—no puny, sad, little corpses buried in the heather.'

Lomax, wanting a respite from Carne, tried to lead the conversation away from him and to his own specialty—beautifully woven Indian dhurries.

'They were woven in the jails in the time of the Raj,' Leary interrupted, airing his knowledge and returning the conversation to where he wanted it. 'Prisons in these days of overcrowding are non-productive. Carne's intelligence will be sadly wasted. I have sympathy for him, but sympathy shouldn't cloud judgment. He's guilty. He shouldn't go free.'

Jacobson, sharing an adjacent table with Quinn, Selina and Elaine, overheard him and knew that Quinn had, too. Quinn had kindly ordered a glass of milk for him and a packet of digestive biscuits when he had declared that he couldn't face the food. Anxiety had killed his appetite. He had voted for Carne's acquittal at the last count without being sure why. On balance it seemed the lesser load to bear on his conscience. 'Freedom,' he said to Quinn, 'is a gift of God. It is better to be charitable than vengeful.' It was a mild version of what he expected Quinn to say to Leary.

Quinn, however, was silent. During the drive to the hotel Leary had made some general remarks about jury nobbling. He had eyed Quinn contemplatively as he had made them. Quinn's rage, tinged heavily with guilt, had been deep and silent like the black levels of the ocean. He was surfacing gradually into a state of calm, helped to some extent by watching the big man opposite him sipping his milk and by listening to Elaine and Selina conversing about health food. Cider vinegar, apparently, was good for you. He forced his mind to concentrate on the mundane and thereby rest it.

The hotel had set aside a small sitting-room on the first floor for the sole use of the jurors, but it was so much like a chintzy version of the jury room that few wanted to stay in it. By ten-thirty Quinn was sitting there alone. He had a strong mental image of Frances at home alone. He could see her lying on Timothy's bed, the radio on the floor by her side, gin or whisky or whatever tipple she hadn't yet consumed on the bedside table.

Her drink problem, though understandable, was acute. One day soon someone would have to do something positive about it. Was that why she had left the state school? Disruptive behaviour had been the term used. The head of the private school had softened it up and called it adolescent instability and blamed changes in the home background. It didn't always follow.

Timothy, as far as he knew, had weathered the break-up between himself and Gretl with reasonable calm. But then the break-up had been amicable and unfussed. With Carne and his wife the alliance must have been uneasy for a long time. Frances had sided with her mother, but her rejection of her father—even now—wasn't total. At the last moment the bond was there. He sensed a deep dependency in her—a dependency that to some degree had been transferred to him. *I think I could love you.* Disturbing words. In her confused immaturity she chose what she wanted to believe. She refused to believe that he bedded Blossom.

Taking Blossom to bed was a delight, but it wasn't just the pleasure of sex. It was being aware of her soft, gentle little body lying beside him asleep in the dark hours. She comforted him. Her word. A good one. She gave generously to anyone who needed her. She was a rare person, uniquely undemanding. In no way had she complicated his life.

As Frances was complicating it.

As the lovely mature Selina would like to complicate it.

Earlier in the evening they had met on the landing outside her bedroom door. She had just returned from the bathroom and was wearing a lightweight cream-coloured coat over her underwear. The coat, not fastened, allowed a glimpse of a dark blue bra and slip. The bath

214

water, she told him, was tepid. 'I suppose if the jury is out for days someone makes a list of necessities—like a face flannel and a toothbrush.' She was talking quickly, nervously. 'How will you men manage to shave in the morning?'

He had told her that there was a disposable razor on his dressing-table. Also a new comb.

'I suppose,' she said, 'there are worse privations than having no night wear.'

Her smile was warm and for a moment she had looked at him squarely and the sexual semaphores were clear.

Received and understood. Or perhaps not fully understood. She wasn't the type, he guessed, to scatter her favours around. If he walked in on her tonight he might be disrupting a marriage. He had done it before. It had been done to him. The survival rate was high. No one had killed anyone as a consequence of it. There had been no corpse on a Welsh mountain. No offspring had become a lush.

When he went up to bed he hesitated momentarily outside her door and then went on to his own room. He had rejected Frances's overtures last night because he had been afraid of her sexual immaturity. Tonight he was rejecting Selina who was both sexually mature and desirable. Why? Because he didn't feel brash enough to tap on her door with a lame and obvious excuse. Because he both liked and respected her. Because at times he could be bloody old-fashioned and this kind of relationship needed a degree of delicacy—a preliminary period of getting to know one another. Selina might be of the future—an attractive possibility. Just now, the present was complex enough.

During the night heavy fingers of rain battered the windows and there were faint rumbles of thunder. Most of the jurors slept through it. Selina awakened and thought of Quinn . . .

All she wanted was a simple act of love with a man who wasn't her husband—and for the first time. She had gone to bed in her slip. Typical modesty, she thought. I am a conditioned, middle-aged married woman. I am so respectable that I shine like the Holy Grail—and so he runs from me. She wished she could pluck up the courage to pursue.

Quinn awoke and hoped that Frances hadn't. The house was too big, too silent, too old to be alone in. If she had boozed herself up to capacity, and she probably had, she might sleep the night through. He began worrying about Carne again. Frances had pushed her father on to his shoulders like a casualty on a battlefield that had to be removed under fire. Unless he was extraordinarily lucky, the flak at some stage would be aimed at him for accepting the load. A fine—or prison—or both? And if the freed

Carne was guilty—what of the parental bond then? A filial lie shouldn't result in a homicidal maniac being returned whole to a daughter who'd done her damn-all best to reject him and then changed her mind.

He sat up in bed and groped for his cigarettes and lighter on the bedside table. Outside he could hear the rumble of traffic, not heavy yet. Dawn was a grey square behind the curtained window. He lit his cigarette and lay back on the pillows inhaling the tobacco smoke and trying to marshal his thoughts constructively. He had done battle with considerable vigour until now. Doubts were born in the night hours—out of fatigue, perhaps. Calm certainty might come with the morning.

Carne, awakened by the storm, awoke to panic. The elements seemed to shred his self-control like a high wind tearing the fabric of a house. He couldn't breathe and believed he was having a heart attack. The ceiling of his cell was too low and the walls were pressing in. He wanted to push and heave and fight. He wanted to run down long corridors and gulp in clear fresh air.

The prison doctor, called from his bed, diagnosed stress. The diagnosis was reassuring only up to a point. To die of heart disease, once the fight for freedom was lost, was neat. A quick and tidy end.

The doctor had told him he could breathe. So

he breathed. Raspingly. Painfully.

The prison officer at the Old Bailey had advised him to take a sedative. He hadn't heeded his advice. The doctor now was insisting that he should swallow a small white pill with a sip of water. He swallowed it and thankfully the walls receded.

He slept again and dreamt of Frances. He didn't know that he cried in his sleep. In the morning he felt shaky and dressing was a problem.

Everyone continued to be kind.

He wondered who would be kind to Frances when she was left on her own. Who would hedge her around with care? He scrutinised his own actions and knew them to be appallingly wrong. Not callously indifferent as the prosecution had alleged. He had distanced himself from the horror in order to survive it, but it was never distant enough. His mind formed pictures, sometimes of events he hadn't seen, and these were the worst. He hadn't been present at the exhumation, but images of it haunted him. The police had taken him to the spot and had watched curiously for his reaction. He had walked away from them, striving to be calm. He hadn't consciously directed his footsteps to the village church, but had found himself there. The church door had been locked. He had needed help. There wasn't any. On the way back to the road, through the church-yard, he had noticed David Mason's grave. David who had died comfortably in his bed and been given a respectable funeral by a woman who had stopped loving him a long time ago, if she had ever been capable of loving him at all.

Olivia's words, spoken a few weeks before the murder, came to him. 'Think how wonderful it would be if nobody gave a damn about anybody. Love is corrosive—like hate. Do you suppose we invited it, Jocelyn and I?'

They had been standing in the village street oblivious of a sudden heavy shower. She had been carrying a loaf of bread and it was getting sodden. Her cheeks were wet with rain and there might have been tears, though he didn't think so. She had turned and left him, her long plait swinging like the tail of an angry cat, and he had watched her walk away from him until she was out of sight.

She had been carefully non-committal in court. Her reticence was self-protective. Had she said more her relationship with Jocelyn might have become clear. Her involvement would have led to embarrassing and difficult questions. On a more mundane level, too, she would be anxious to avoid undue attention. A sexual deviant in a small Welsh village would do less well with her crafts business than a grieving widow. He wondered if she would be in court to hear the verdict.

Hester, he was sure, would be there. Jocelyn, in a rare moment of censure, had called her a most dangerous woman. Jocelyn was right.

Jocelyn.

He was able to say her name.

He was able to see her.

Not murdered.

Jocelyn as she was. An unsatisfactory wife. A loving mother.

As he was driven to the Old Bailey she felt as close to him as if she were seated beside him in the prison van. There was no longer any menace in her presence. He could almost feel the skin of her hand under his palm. He closed his fingers gently.

*　　　*　　　*

The jurors, back in the jury room, looked at the familiar surroundings without enthusiasm. The hotel breakfast hadn't been much better than the dinner of the night before. Jacobson, by now extremely hungry, had given his bacon to Quinn and Quinn had given him his fried egg in return. Conversation tended to be strained. The jurors with a conscience, and most of them had one in varying degrees, were worried about the verdict.

The previous evening, after several hours of debate, they had asked for the judge's ruling on a majority verdict. It would be acceptable, he had told them, if after a further period of

220

discussion they failed to agree, but the majority had to be at least ten to two. They hoped they would reach that figure today.

'We didn't ask to judge him,' Lomax was heard saying plaintively to Professor Leary; 'jury duty should be voluntary. Surely there are many people who'd be glad to do it. I'm not one of them.'

Leary was and it wasn't necessary to say so. He made an appropriate remark about every citizen's duty. 'Ladies and gentlemen, after a good night's rest, our minds should be so much clearer. Let us apply ourselves once more.'

The 'ladies and gentlemen' jarred. They might be 'ladies and gentlemen' to the court officials, they were this man's colleagues. Christian names were being used by some. They had all put up with the awkwardness of a night's stay at a hotel without hand-luggage. Irene Sinclair's feet had swollen and she hadn't any diuretic tablets with her. She had swopped her shoes with Elaine Balfour, who wore shoes with adjustable straps. Cornwallis had run out of pipe tobacco and Middler had given him a packet of chewing gum to curb the craving. Trina's dress zip had stuck, Sarah unzipped it. If Professor Leary had needed aid of any kind he would have been given it. Whether he liked it or not he was one of them. They looked at him without approval as he began to list all the reasons why Carne should be sent down.

They looked to Quinn for a rebuttal and today he gave it with less force. He was tired and uncertain. He wasn't sure what his thoughts were. It would be so much easier to call a halt to the proceedings by declaring his involvement than to keep going over old ground.

'A conviction based on circumstantial evidence,' he said, 'is never satisfactory. But that's all we've got. We're convinced, one way or the other, without proof. I can't think of anything else that might push us along towards a verdict. I just don't know what other argument there is.'

'I think I do,' Selina spoke out, surprising herself and everyone else. She was normally reticent. She didn't care about Carne all that deeply, but she cared about Quinn. If she could woo him with words then she'd find the right ones.

'It might seem nonsense to speak of instinct,' she said, 'but I'm going to do just that. We all remember Hester Allendale's performance in court. She believed Carne was guilty, she said, and she touched her head and her heart—here and here.' Selina touched herself in the same places. 'I don't know what you thought, but she didn't convince me. I think she was lying. I can talk about sensing Carne's innocence without making any dramatic gestures. You have that feeling about some people. You know there's no violence in them. You can't write down reasons

222

on a piece of paper. I've seen that man's programmes so many times—some of them are trite, I grant you—but we're not judging what he's given to do. We're judging him—and for me, anyway, he comes over convincingly.'

She paused, hesitated. She was beginning to believe what she was saying. She *did* believe it. 'In court he has been very cool and restrained. I'm sure I could sense guilt in a guilty person. I don't sense it in him. Not at all.'

She turned to Elaine Balfour. 'Elaine doesn't either and neither does Trina. Both Elaine and I have had the experience of years—Trina has the intuituion of youth. Sarah, I feel, wants to admit to what her instinct tells her is right. She told me earlier this morning that she was worried about a guilty verdict. I think if we have another show of hands she might be with us.'

She smiled at Irene Sinclair. 'Irene's the most gentle person I know. She would never commit a man to prison for life unless she was positive beyond doubt that he was guilty. It must be the most awful burden a juryman or woman can have to know that you're responsible for the loss of an innocent man's freedom.'

Lastly she turned to Quinn. Her face, bare of make-up, was flushed. 'You,' she said, not using his name but making 'you' sound warmly intimate, 'feel as I do. You've put it more clearly than I ever can. If I read you correctly, and I think I do, you'll take root here rather than return a verdict of guilty. And so will I.' She made a sweeping gesture with her hand taking in everyone at the table. 'None of you,' she said, 'will force me away from what I believe to be right. I will not leave this jury room to return a verdict of guilty. I will not have that man on my conscience. If we argue for ever I will not change.'

Quinn, startled and amused, looked down at the empty sheet of paper he had been folding and re-folding as she spoke. It hadn't occurred to him to use an emotive argument coupled with the awful threat of staying in this dreadful room for ever. He wondered if her speech would have been more or less ardent if they had made love to each other last night. Justice shouldn't balance so precariously on the axis of sexual attraction.

The women, surprised to be marshalled under Selina's banner, saw no reason to desert her. What she said was true. You condemned with no evidence, or you acquitted with no evidence. According to the judge, guilt had to be proved. It couldn't be. If a small cold voice in the back of your head told you that Carne was guilty, it was muted by Selina's warm vibrant voice speaking of your gentleness and intuition. You needed to think well of yourself after this day. If you awoke in the small hours you didn't want the hideous trivia of anxiety to be made more real by knowing you'd put Carne in a prison cell.

There were more practical reasons, too:

Sarah had her period. The first day was always the worst. She wanted to lie down.

Irene's neighbour wouldn't take kindly to being neighbourly for very long. Taking care of her sister was a charitable act that should have a reasonable time limit.

Trina's crowned tooth had become loose when she had bitten a hard piece of toast at breakfast. She needed immediate dental attention or she'd lose it.

Elaine's bedroom window hadn't been securely fastened. Last night's heavy rain would have seeped in. If not seen to there would be a stain on the living-room ceiling.

Most of the men, too, had practical reasons for not wanting to protract the discussion. Middler was particularly anxious to get back to his clinic. Jacobson was concerned about his family trying to cope without him. The snack-bar was in a rough area. His presence was needed.

Professor Leary was the only jury member who was totally objective and totally dedicated. 'Mrs McKay,' he said to Selina, 'whilst appreciating your obviously strong feelings in this case, I must warn you not to let concern for the accused overrule your common sense. Jocelyn Carne is dead. The most likely murderer is her husband. We cannot overlook

225

the obvious. To speak of instinct is nonsense. You are surely too intelligent to close your mind to rational argument.'

Cornwallis spoke bitterly before she could answer. 'And so we pin our butts,' he said, 'to the ruddy chairs—while you, lady, and you, sir, argue till the cows come home.' He had arranged to service a customer's central heating boiler in the afternoon. There seemed little chance now of arriving in time. His anger was growing by the minute.

'It's not a closed shop,' Quinn said mildly, returning to the fray. 'I'm firmly on Mrs McKay's side, as you know. And so are most of you. How about an immediate show of hands?'

This time, all the five women together with Jacobson, Cornwallis and Middler voted with him for an acquittal. The votes were expedient in some cases, but Quinn wasn't questioning motives. Nine to three. He began concentrating on Lomax and Dalton. Leary, he knew, would never be budged.

Lomax, anxious to attend an auction of Persian rugs, struggled silently with his conscience. Dalton, rubbed raw by argument, tried unsuccessfully to keep calm. In a normal environment his nervous tension didn't show. Here it was exacerbated. In an outburst that shocked everyone he stated his feelings.

'He battered his wife's head in. You've seen the forensic model. Carne, the super-star—

226

Carne, the super-Brit! Carne, the self-complacent, bloody murderer! If there was any justice in this sick and feeble land, he would be executed. Hanged. Electrocuted. Shot. Whatever method. It doesn't matter. But dead.' He began to shake.

Leary, like the other jurors, was troubled. Dalton was unbalanced—a dangerous man to have on a jury. 'The verdict,' he told him, 'should be based on clear thinking. In your case there's strong animosity. Your judgment is no more valid than Mrs McKay's. You're both emotionally motivated.'

Lomax agreed. 'If it can't be proved by reasoned argument,' he said, 'then I think I prefer a verdict of non-proven. And as that's only valid in the Scottish courts, I'll change sides and go for an acquittal. As for this "sick and feeble land",' he added, 'we may err on the side of mercy and that's no bad thing.'

'Your patriotism is commendable,' Dalton said sarcastically, 'but spare me a spiel on Christian charity.' There was a carafe of water on the table and he poured himself a drink. 'We all carry memories,' he said, 'and we all have our prejudices.' He gulped the water. 'During the trouble in Rhodesia—I beg your pardon, *Zimbabwe*—' the emphasis was caustic, 'I returned to my home to find my wife and eldest son slaughtered. It happened in a small copse at the back of the property. There was blood on a carob tree—their decapitated bodies were under it. I hacked the tree down. As I smashed my axe into it, I wasn't smashing into the bark of a tree.' He returned the tumbler to the table. 'You understand what I'm telling you?'

His hands were still shaking and he pushed them into his jacket pocket. 'Carne is here. We have him. When we talk of retribution it means something. I know there's no racial or political link with Carne—but there's the link of a brutal killing. I can't separate the two images in my mind. Of course I'm emotionally motivated. Wouldn't you be?'

The silence was broken by a few awkward phrases of understanding and condolence, cut short by Dalton's expression of contempt.

'I'm not asking for your sympathy—I'm explaining my position—why I'm not returning a verdict of not guilty. *I cannot do it.* You'll do what you feel you must. I can't keep arguing about it. I can't be calm about this. As from now I'm saying no more. He should be convicted. If you're too feeble-minded to see that, I can't force you to see it. It's up to you.'

'It seems we have the right numbers for a majority verdict,' Quinn pointed out quietly. 'I suggest we settle for it.'

There was a general murmur of assent.

Leary frowned. 'If that's what we decide,' he said, 'Carne will have been well served, but British justice will not.' He eyed the jurors with

228

extreme displeasure. Quinn, with his twisted intelligence, had waged a personal war against him. It was his nature to be contrary. The women, with the exception of Mrs McKay, were vacillatory. And so were the men—apart from Dalton who had been made paranoid by grief. Until now, he had had a deep respect for the British judicial system. No more. If these people were representative of all juries then the guilty walked free and—worse—the innocent were punished. 'We would have wasted less time,' he said, 'if we had tossed a coin at the commencement. Is there anything I can say to convince you that we ourselves are guilty of dereliction of duty if we quit at this point?'

'There is nothing you can say,' Selina tried not to sound triumphant. 'But if you find it too difficult to go against your conscience and declare a majority verdict of not guilty, then perhaps you would like Mr Quinn to take over as foreman?'

It was her gift to Quinn. She hoped the professor would allow her to make it.

'Very well,' he said shortly. In this particular instance the law was an ass. Quinn could bray rather better than he could—so let him get on with it.

Before the jury bailiff was contacted, Leary indicated the *Notice to Members of the Jury* pinned on the wall. 'You will permit me,' he said, putting on his glasses, 'to read it to you:

229

"Her Majesty's Judges remind you of the solemn obligations upon you not to reveal in any circumstances, to any person, either during the trial or after it is over, anything relating to it which has occurred in this room while you have been considering your verdict."'

His voice was heavy with censure. 'It occurs to me that the rule has been well kept in the past. Had it not been so, the fallibility of the system would have become obvious. However, let us perpetuate the myth. May the public continue to believe, erroneously, in our common sense and integrity.'

The jury, aware that there was some truth in the rebuke, but nevertheless annoyed by it, waited to be escorted back to court.

Quinn caught Selina's eye and smiled. 'A celebration dinner,' he suggested, 'some time during the week?'

She had been hoping for a celebration dinner today. He told her it wasn't possible and they exchanged telephone numbers.

Today belonged to Frances.

And to Carne.

In a more minor way, it belonged to him. He had done what Frances had wanted him to do and had got away with it. There should be some degree of satisfaction, if not euphoria. So why this feeling of unease?

CHAPTER FOURTEEN

'Your client,' Breddon said to McNair, 'looks like Lazarus emerging from the charnel house—astonished.'

McNair grinned. The verdict might not have been expected, but it was popular. There had been a murmur of approval in the public gallery which Spencer-Leigh hadn't bothered to silence. McNair wondered what the judge's personal reaction was; if he had felt any surprise at the verdict he had been careful not to show it. He had thanked the jury and then turned to Carne and graciously dismissed him.

McNair, saying something about succouring the newly-arisen, went over to Carne who was standing bemused, uncertain what to do next. People he didn't know were pressing in on him. Mouths were smiling. The hisses and yowls had become serenades of sweetness. His public was telling him that he was much loved. Hands that a day or two ago would have pushed him gladly into the pit were now squeezing his with warmth and delight.

He was free. Did that mean he could just walk out? Or did he have to sign something first? Was it raining out there in the world—or did the sun shine?

He could see Hester Allendale pushing

through the crowd towards the exit. No one attempted to speak to her. Her fans, if they were present, had cooled in their ardour.

Where was Olivia? In bitter retreat, too? Would she let matters lie? Possibly. She'd be too fearful of him to do otherwise. Someone had been in the vicinity when he'd buried Jocelyn. He'd heard footfalls—sensed a presence—and then dismissed it as imagination. It had been David, of course. Anyone else would have gone to the police. David was the only witness who would see and not condemn. Jocelyn had threatened his marriage, his hatred of her was intense. It was in his nature to go away and say nothing. And then, finally, in the weakness of his last illness his conscience must have troubled him—or Olivia had goaded him—and he'd told her. A startling declaration on his deathbed: 'I know where your lover's body is buried, Olivia. She's been dead a long time. Not pretty any more.' Or had he told her more gently? Perhaps in the final weeks there had been more understanding between them—even affection.

Carne wished he could stop thinking about it. It was over. Finished. He should feel at peace, not stifled and claustrophobic. There were too many people here. Too much noise. He said vaguely to anyone who might be listening, 'I can't . . .' It was a general negation. I can't cope. I can't move in any direction.

McNair put his hand lightly on his arm.

'Come and sit for a bit. You need to get your breath.' He followed McNair to the barristers' table. It felt strange being in the well of the court—a different perspective. The dock looked large like the prow of a ship.

'Well,' McNair said, 'the ordeal is over. Felicitations.'

'What? Oh, thank you—yes. I mean, thank *you*.'

'Don't let's kid ourselves,' McNair went on crisply, 'you gave me a tough brief and I just about managed to chew the corners of it. You had a sympathetic jury.'

'A majority verdict.'

'Don't question the gods when they bestow gifts.'

'But you question the verdict?'

'Nonsense, I'm delighted.' McNair looked at him keenly. 'You'll be badgered by the press just as soon as you step out of here. You need a clear head for them. How do you feel?'

Feel? Calmer now that he was away from the crowds. His brain had stopped making pictures. The screen was a dull grey. He said he felt all right.

'Good—but take it easy for a bit. I'll go and disrobe and I'll be back in twenty minutes or so.'

*　　　*　　　*

233

Quinn waited until McNair had gone and the court-room cleared of its officers and spectators. Then he went over to Frances's father and introduced himself. 'Robert Quinn—the jury foreman.'

Carne remembered him very clearly. The 'Not guilty' had been delivered in ringing tones with almost thespian panache, but the glance he had shot him afterwards had been speculative. Had he been one of the dissenting jurors? He was standing in front of him now, not smiling. No hand extended to grasp his with warm congratulation. No honeyed words.

He told Quinn he was indebted to him. It was a polite assumption.

More than you know, Quinn thought, seating himself beside him. 'Last night,' he said, 'the votes were loaded against you. This morning matters improved.'

Carne was puzzled. 'You've come to tell me this?'

'No—just a matter of passing interest. I've come to tell you that Frances is physically well but emotionally very troubled. For the last couple of weeks she has been living with four young buskers at my home. I can take you to her now—if you want me to. She may not want me to. I'm risking that. I think it's necessary for her to see you. What she does afterwards is up to her.'

Carne's flesh felt as if it had suddenly frozen

over his bones. 'What has she told you?'

A pertinent question, Quinn thought, and you've gone rigid with fear. He hadn't expected to feel this degree of contempt. The unease that he had begun to experience during the night became stronger. He answered honestly, 'That you're a bastard. I'm sorry—but if you're expecting a loving reconciliation you're not going to get one.'

Carne very slowly relaxed and then, to Quinn's surprise, he smiled.

Quinn told him where his car was parked. 'It's a green Saab—S registration—if you can get yourself to it without half of Fleet Street hanging around you, I'll be ready to drive off.'

He read Carne's expression correctly, 'And if you're wondering why the hell I've got myself involved in all this, I've been asking myself the same question ever since the trial began.'

The alleged re-appearance of Frances concentrated Carne's mind wonderfully. It took him forty minutes of expert elusive action, abetted by McNair, to reach Quinn's car. Quinn, on the alert for him, opened the door swiftly when he saw the Bentley slowing down. With a quick word of thanks to McNair, Carne sprinted across the road and got in beside Quinn.

Quinn, keeping his head averted from McNair's curious glance, drove off. 'Who did you tell him I was?'

'A journalist acquaintance.'

'Credible. At one time it would have been true. A promise of an exclusive story, I suppose? How much am I supposed to be paying you?'

'Not discussed.' Carne added drily: 'It has occurred to me, of course, that there might be a cash flow in the other direction.'

'Put your mind at rest,' Quinn said without rancour. 'I'm not one of the criminal fraternity. Frances really is there. By now she'll have heard the news of the acquittal on the radio.'

Lunch-time traffic was heavy and Quinn concentrated on his driving.

'How far?' Carne asked him.

'We should be home shortly after one.'

★   ★   ★

Home, Carne discovered when they reached the quiet, sleazy side-street of Edwardian houses, was not the kind of environment he had bought by sweat, toil and professional charm for Jocelyn and Frances. He looked curiously at the dead-eyed windows, some draped with nets, and wondered about the devious and twisted pathways that had brought Frances here. Until now he hadn't allowed his mind to dwell on her whereabouts. She had been out there somewhere—fending for herself as best she could. Who was this law-breaking juryman, he wondered, who had given her refuge? He wasn't

236

young—in his late thirties—so his behaviour could not be explained away as the impulsive action of youth.

Quinn drew up near the corner. 'My house is down on the other side. Frances might not notice the car if we stop here. I think we should talk.'

Impatient to see her, Carne nevertheless restrained himself as best he could. 'You told me she was well—what else is there to say?'

'She has a drink problem.'

He nearly said, 'Is that all?' but stopped himself in time. 'I know. She's already had a period of drying out. I'll see that she gets proper care.'

A cool admission, Quinn thought. Drying out? At her age? Jesus! At what age had she started becoming a lush? At fourteen? Fifteen? And *why?* He had believed it to be recent—a result of stress. What sort of home background was it? How long had the pain been going on?

'If she opts not to return with you, then my home is hers for as long as she wants it.' It had to be said.

Carne felt a surge of quite irrational jealousy. 'Have you slept with her?'

'No.'

'So it isn't a sexual relationship?'

'Would you expect it to be?'

Carne side-stepped it. 'The other young people you spoke about—the buskers—is she

237

...' he tried to find the right words, 'emotionally involved with one of them?'

'No.'

'It's a bizarre set-up. I don't understand it.' Carne was aware that the car was smelling of petrol and he felt a slight nausea. He rolled down the window. 'The fact that you've harboured her and stayed on the jury might invalidate the trial.' The possibility was frightening.

Quinn dismissed it. 'She hasn't flaunted her presence. We're not exactly neighbourly hereabouts. The buskers know what I'm doing is illegal—but they're not great lovers of the law: they won't talk. I decided to keep quiet and serve on the jury to help her. I just hope I've helped in the right way. Most of the time my conscience is clear; by that I mean I'm totally untroubled by the effect my actions might have—unless someone vulnerable gets hurt. Frances is vulnerable.'

'I love my daughter.' The words sounded cold—a private emotion deeply felt but grudgingly expressed.

Quinn looked at him, weighed the words in his mind and believed them.

'She blames you for her mother's lesbianism.'

Carne was startled. 'So she told you about Jocelyn and Olivia?'

'She described the relationship as grotesque. A shocked over-reaction. My guess is that she hadn't known about it very long.'

Someone in the neighbourhood was burning rubbish in one of the back yards. Billows of black, gritty smoke swept over the roof-tops scattering ash. A dirty fire. The burning cottage had smelt much the same, Carne remembered. Acrid. A consuming of old fabric. He had described it differently to Frances. A crisp, clean smell, bright yellow flames. Soporific, stupid words to someone out of her mind with grief.

He wondered what else she had told this juryman.

'If she decides to go back with you today,' Quinn said, 'then she must make the decision freely. She knows what happened in the cottage. She's kept all the facts from me. Yesterday morning, when there could have been a showdown before I left for court, she made off somewhere. I would have pressed for the truth yesterday. She probably knew that.'

Carne was silent. Frances was good at making off. She found lairs in odd places, such as this, and crouched in solitude.

Quinn watched smuts from the fire speckling the windscreen. 'She asked me to do what I could for you—in a note. On the strength of that I brought what influence I could to bear on the other jurors. Perhaps unwisely. I don't know. I keep remembering that she refused to give evidence on your behalf. You needed her in

239

court. She didn't go.'

The billows of smoke were thinning into blue streamers against the afternoon sun. A large shaggy mongrel bounded out of one of the houses and loped down the street. An old man with a built-up surgical shoe hobbled after it. They disappeared around the corner and the street was empty again.

'She eluded the police,' Quinn went on, 'in case she was forced to appear for the prosecution. She's ambivalent towards you. I don't know what's going on inside her head. Perhaps she never intended seeing you again. But I don't think so. I have the feeling she *needs* to see you. She's still her parents' child. Not her own woman yet.' He grimaced. It sounded like trash psychology dished up in an agony column, but he couldn't think how else to put it. 'I want you to meet—in my presence. All my concern is for her and what is best for her.'

'Your concern is laudable,' Carne said stiffly, 'but if you're keeping me here in your car to try to discover if I'm a fit person to repossess my own daughter, then I suggest you're wasting your time. That's something that only she can know.'

'Not repossess,' Quinn emphasised. 'Reassure—if you can. Heal—if possible.' He put the car in gear and drove half-way down the street and then he stopped and got out. 'That's it. That's my house.'

Carne looked at the peeling paint work and then at the pot of flowers by the front door. Somebody had bothered to pretty the place up a bit. The environment didn't fit Quinn. He couldn't understand why he should have landed in it. Nor could he understand his underlying tenderness for Frances. She wasn't a pretty girl. She had no gift to charm. Never once had she brought a boy-friend home. But this man—this stranger—was fond of her.

He followed Quinn over the cemented area to the front door and then as he was about to put the key in the lock he answered the question that Quinn had been careful not to ask. 'The past doesn't threaten the present—or the future. I appreciate your concern for Frances. She will be safe in my care.'

Quinn nodded. He said nothing. There was nothing to say.

In the cool shadows of the hall a single Slipper Orchid glowed white and purple behind cellophane on the telephone table. 'Not one of yours—bought specially for you—happy belated birthday' was written on a piece of white card propped against it. In place of a signature was a crudely drawn flower. So Blossom was home.

Timothy's parcel had arrived and had lost some of the packing in transit. It was on the shelf under the table. Quinn, glancing at it quickly, saw part of a coiled pot, painted a lurid green, obviously made by Timothy. He resisted the temptation to strip off the rest of the paper to see if it was intact. He was pleased with both gifts. Later the beautiful orchid would be put into the hideous pot, and he would admire them at his leisure.

He was about to take Frances's father down the passageway into the living-room when he became aware that Frances was walking down the stairs. She had recently bathed and smelt of talcum powder. Her small stubby feet were white with it and left imprints on the dark brown stair carpet. She was walking with great care as if there was a chasm down below—or the maw of a volcano. Her eyes were on her father's, her face a stiff mask of control. Quinn wondered how drunk she was—or was she drunk at all?

On the bottom step she paused.

Carne, fighting back tears, stood still—waiting.

She nodded once—twice—as if the scene had been set in her mind and was now being played to her satisfaction. 'You said they'd aquit you.'

'Yes,' Carne said.

She stepped down, took three paces towards him, and rested her head against his chest. He made no move to kiss her—touch her.

She moved back from him. 'I've washed my hair.'

It was still wet—thick and coarse. She was so like her mother it was almost unbearable.

'And I'm wearing borrowed clothes.'

Carne looked at her yellow cotton dress, too tight across the breasts. The last time she had worn borrowed clothes had been at the cottage. Jocelyn's matronly green striped silk had accommodated her breasts with inches to spare. Her own jeans and shirt had been stuffed into a linen bag and pushed under the sink.

It was an unacceptable memory, the kind that dried his throat.

'I've scrubbed my nails,' Frances held her hands out for inspection. 'See.'

The pattern was duplicating itself. Carne's heart lurched into over-drive. He didn't answer.

She turned to Quinn. 'Blossom came home last night.'

Puzzled by dimly sensed terror, overlaid by talk of cleansing rituals, Quinn was silent.

'She wanted to be with me for the verdict,' Frances said. 'But there wasn't a verdict, so she comforted me in your bed. She's there now. You'd better go to her.'

It wasn't, Quinn realised, a suggestion that he should go and make love.

He took the stairs two at a time.

* * *

Blossom was lying on the side of the bed she always lay on when she came to him. The herb pillow she used to bring had split open and pungent herbs mixed with coagulated blood in

243

her wounds. She had stopped bleeding several hours ago and there had been a lot of blood. Her lacerations were like Jocelyn's lacerations—a mad battering of the head. Her dark hair was a storm around her face, but her mouth was strangely tranquil, lips slightly parted. Her sightless eyes, wide open, looked deeply into his. You must forgive her, she seemed to be saying, once more and finally, she knows not what she does.

Shock, rage, grief, thrust Quinn down into hell. His body was sweating and burning as he reached out and touched her forehead, pale and cold as shattered onyx. Flecks of lavender stuck to his finger-tips.

Somewhere behind him, breaking through the high-pitched whine in his ears, he could hear Frances babbling to her father.

'I didn't mean to. Any more than I meant to with Mummy. It happened too quickly. I couldn't stop it. I needed a drink. She hadn't touched me in bed until then. I was getting out to fetch one. But she put her arms around me and held me. She said drinking did no good. She seemed so strong. And then I stopped trying to get away from her. I began to feel what Mummy must have felt for Olivia. She was corrupting me. Kissing me. Stroking me. I saw Mummy all over again in my mind—the night she told me about Olivia. And then everything began to scream inside me—like it did then—and I hit her and hit her and hit her.'

Quinn turned around from the bed.

Frances and her father were standing at the bedroom door. Carne had his hands on Frances's shoulders and was holding her protectively against him. He had survived the ordeal of the trial without obvious physical trauma, but in the last few minutes his skin had become livid with premature aging.

Frances twisted in his grasp so that she spoke directly to him and not to Quinn.

'She's not as stiff as Mummy was. She hasn't been dead so long. After I phoned you about Mummy you were hours coming. This happened during the night.' Her voice became sharply urgent. 'I don't know where you'll put her. Robert's garden is paved. But there's soil in the orchid house and it isn't hard to dig.'

Carne, fearing Quinn's reaction, held her closer. 'Don't hurt her,' he pleaded, 'please.' And then, 'I'm sorry—oh, dear God, I'm sorry.'

Had Quinn a child of his own, he wondered? Did he know what it was to love—to act on impulse and without reason to protect someone who didn't give a damn for you most of the time, but who meant more to you than anyone else? Her mental instability, Jocelyn had said to him bitterly, must have stemmed from him. Over the last months he had come to believe that it must be true. He should have listened to the medical advice he and Jocelyn had been given in the past. Not just a drink problem, they had been told. More than that. She had needed expert care. He had been enraged. Jocelyn, calmer than he, had been prepared to listen. He had overruled her. Let Frances be. She's all right. She's a child. She'll grow out of it. She's normal. Normal.

And so was he. She'd murdered Jocelyn and he'd buried Jocelyn. It would be normal to kill Quinn before he phoned the police. The thought came and went.

Quinn's left foot touched the broken remains of a table lamp. Blossom must have tried to wrench it from her. Her small hand on the brown checked duvet was cut across the palm. Gentle, fragile, heterosexual Blossom who had made a loving gesture to the wrong person at the wrong time.

There was dried blood on the telephone by the bed. It took Quinn several minutes to control his fingers sufficiently to dial the police. Even now, he doubted if Carne would have done it.

Frances, amazed, appalled, by this ultimate treachery, looked from one man to the other. 'You can't,' she said to Quinn, 'you've got to help me. You can't do this!'

And to her father, 'Daddy, stop him!'

Carne's arm was across her breasts, pinning her to him as she squirmed to break free. 'No,' he said gently.

He listened as Quinn gave details of the murder.

A murder that he and Quinn between them had helped to commit.

Earlier Carne had felt an irrational jealousy of him, but this now had given way to blazing anger, barely controlled. Frances was his daughter—his responsibility—she belonged to no one else. You trespassed on my patch, juryman. Am I supposed to thank you for what you've done? If you hadn't taken her into your home this wouldn't have happened. Had you got yourself off the jury, it wouldn't have happened. You would have been here last night. With or without you I would have been acquitted of her mother's murder ... or, perhaps not. Either way that Chinese girl would be alive and Frances would be free.

God damn you for what you've done!

Frances had stopped struggling and had begun to shiver. She was very frightened. He spoke to her soothingly, tenderly. She said she was cold.

He noticed a towelling dressing-gown of Quinn's hanging over a chair. The blood hadn't splashed this far and it looked clean and warm. He took it and wrapped it around her.

It was a visual statement of care. Of dual responsibility. Both men were aware of it. Neither commented.

Quinn watched Carne preceding him with

Frances down the stairs. His hands as he had put the dressing-gown around her had been gentle. As they walked he was carefully holding up the hem so that she wouldn't fall.

He was too suffused with hatred to sit with father and daughter in the living-room and wait for the police. Neither could he bear to stay in the bedroom with Blossom. His grief was too raw and the feeling of responsibility for her death too unbearable. He went down to the hall and prowled around restlessly. Mechanically, not fully aware of what he was doing, he began to strip the rest of the paper from Timothy's present. The feel of the pot was calming. Uneven coils of green clay carefully put together and glazed. He concentrated on it as Timothy must have concentrated on it. He held it as Timothy had held it.

It was a contact. Something he needed. He began to understand Carne.

In the living-room Carne was holding Frances's hand. She was sitting silently beside him on the sofa. In the terrible hiatus before the police arrived there was nothing to be done, nothing to be said. Carne wished he could live the future for her as he had lived the past. He wished out of the depths of his love for her that she had never been born.